PENGUIN BOOKS

CUTS

Malcolm Bradbury is a novelist, critic, television dramatist and part-time Professor of American Studies at the University of East Anglia. He is the author of six novels – *Eating People Is Wrong* (1959), *Stepping Westward* (1965), *The History Man* (1975), which won the Royal Society of Literature Heinemann Prize and was adapted as a famous television series, *Rates of Exchange* (1983), which was shortlisted for the Booker Prize, *Cuts: A Very Short Novel* (1987) and *Doctor Criminale* (1992). All are published by Penguin. His critical works include *The Modern American Novel* (1984, rev. edn. 1992), *No, Not Bloomsbury* (essays, 1987), *The Modern World: Ten Great Writers* (Penguin 1989) and *From Puritanism to Postmodernism: A History of American Literature* (with Richard Ruland, Penguin 1993). His newest work is *The Modern British Novel* (1993), which is forthcoming in Penguin. He has also edited *The Penguin Book of Modern British Short Stories* (1988) and *Modernism* (with James McFarlane, Penguin 1991). He is the author of *Who Do You Think You Are?* (Penguin 1993), a collection of seven stories and nine parodies, and several works of humour and satire, including *Why Come to Slaka?* (Penguin 1992), *Unsent Letters* and *Mensonge* (Penguin 1993).

He has written several television 'novels', including *The Gravy Train* and *The Gravy Train Goes East*. Other television series include adaptations of Tom Sharpe's *Porterhouse Blue* and Kingsley Amis's *The Green Man*. He lives in Norwich, travels a good deal, and in 1991 was awarded the CBE.

MALCOLM BRADBURY

CUTS

PENGUIN BOOKS

To Brian Eastman

PENGUIN BOOKS

Published by the Penguin Group
Penguin Books Ltd, 27 Wrights Lane, London W8 5TZ, England
Penguin Books USA Inc., 375 Hudson Street, New York, New York 10014, USA
Penguin Books Australia Ltd, Ringwood, Victoria, Australia
Penguin Books Canada Ltd, 10 Alcorn Avenue, Toronto, Ontario, Canada M4V 3B2
Penguin Books (NZ) Ltd, 182–190 Wairau Road, Auckland 10, New Zealand

Penguin Books Ltd, Registered Offices: Harmondsworth, Middlesex, England

First published by Hutchinson 1987
Published in Penguin Books 1994
1 3 5 7 9 10 8 6 4 2

Copyright © Malcolm Bradbury, 1987
All rights reserved

Printed in England by Clays Ltd, St Ives plc

1

It was the summer of 1986, and everywhere there were cuts. Every morning, when you opened the morning newspaper – if, that is, you read the serious ones, the ones where the brave reporters went out of the office every day and over the razor-sharp barbed wire to come back with something that more or less resembled news – 'cut' was the most common noun, 'cut' was the most regular verb. They were incising heavy industry, they were slicing steel, they were – by no longer cutting much coal – cutting coal. They were axing the arts, slimming the sciences, cutting inflation and the external services of the BBC. They were reducing public expenditure, bringing down interest rates, eliminating over-production and unnecessary jobs. Ministers were cutting the ribbon to open small new stretches of motorway; in the Treasury they were cutting their coats according to their cloths. They were chopping at the schools, hewing away at the universities, scissoring at the health service, sculpting the hospitals, shutting down operating theatres – so that, in one sense at least, there were actually far *fewer* cuts than before. They were whittling away at waste, slashing out at superfluity, excising rampant excess. There were some people who said they were cutting the country in two – the north from the south, the rich from the poor. There were others, mostly the ones who had themselves been cut, who complained that the cuts were a kind of national hara-kiri, the self-mutilation of a country in its ultimate stage of decline. There were yet others, mostly those who had done quite a lot of the cutting, and who now wanted to see their taxes cut, who explained that it had all been a form of healthy surgery, an elimination of waste, rot and canker, and that the country would be better, much better, than it had been before.

All this was helped by the useful ambiguity of the handy word 'cut'. To trim, to hew, to prune, to shape; to pierce, to incise, to gash, to stab; to mow, to carve, to whittle, to sculpt; to reduce, to curtail, to disbranch, to eliminate; to slash, to geld, to dismember, to castrate; to delete, to assemble, to improve, to edit, as with a book or a film; to ignore, to avoid, to pass by, to pretend not to know at all – all these are just some of the many interesting and various meanings of the elusive word 'cut'.

So it was, that summer of 1986, a time for purpose, for realism, for burnishing and cleansing, for doing away with far too much of this and a wasteful excess of that. It was a time for getting rid of the old soft illusions, and replacing them with the new hard illusions. Realism was back in philosophy and economics, in commerce and commodities, and in paintings and plays, poems and novels – though from novels it had only just begun to leave anyway. It was a time for enterprise, for commercial adventure, for communal capitalism, for opportunity, and more people were buying shares than ever before. And everyone was growing leaner and cleaner, keener and meaner, for after all in a time of cuts it is better to be tough than tender, much more hardware than software. The people who used to talk art now talked only money, and they murmured of the texture of Telecom, the lure of Britoil, the glamour of gas. They got

out of Japan and into Europe, out of offshore and into
unit trusts. In money, only in money, were there
fantasies and dreams, and though work had been cut
there was somehow quite a lot of money about. For what
is pruned here usually springs up there, this being what
happens when you cut things; and this was a summer of
market forces, consumer capitalism, heavy trading,
mergers and takeovers. Everyone you sat down with at
dinner was a company or a conglomerate, a partnership
or a p.l.c., a gnome in Zurich or a name at Lloyd's, if, that
is, they were not out of work. One was usually the one or
the other, that summer of the cuts.

They were cutting clothes that year, neat edgy clothes
that came from the busy High Street designer revolution:
the lapels and the shoulderpads were as sharp as knives
on the suits of the lady accountants who sat in the clean-
cut offices, giving their advice on when to cut and thrust,
when to cut and run. They were cutting hair, plain flat-
top styles of hair that, apart from the odd fancy slavetail,
gave people the military, trimmed look of the austere and
moral Fifties, which were coming back. They were
cutting out smoking, cutting down drinking; everyone
had a bottle of Perrier on the restaurant table that
summer, if they went out to lunch at all. For they were
cutting down flab by cutting out food; that was the
summer of jogging executives in Adidas sweatbands and
of *cuisine minceur*, illustrated food, abstract sauceboat
pictures without much content. They were cutting
wasteful entertaining by fitting in hard-working break-
fasts at the Connaught; that was where a lot of business
was done that year. They were cutting out sex, and
fornication, when practised, grew very staccato and
short, for women now had so much to do. In any case sex

transmitted mortal diseases, much as Egyptian hotels were once thought to do. It was wise not to touch someone who might have touched someone else who in turn had touched someone else. Serial monogamy was in, sex was being replaced by gender, and women who had once talked of love now talked only of sexual harassment. But money was sexy, very sexy. It was the summer of fiscal foreplay, with the prospect in the autumn of the Big Bang. Women in black suits with bright red stockings practised their serial monogamy with young men in Turnbull and Asser shirts, red scarves and blue loden coats who shaved with cut-throat razors and had river-view flats in Wapping, a silver Porsche, and a part-interest in a small vineyard on the Côtes de Gascogne. In designer flats they talked, over the fafafel, of financing a film, buying a time-share in the Seychelles, investing in a piece of a snooker-player, and getting divorced.

It was, in its way, a quiet summer. The number of foreign tourists was severely cut, because of the fear of terrorism and a cut in the value of the dollar. This rather cut down the number of plays and the sales of books, except for remainders, which at cut-price sold very well. There was a Royal Wedding, the prospect of an East-West summit, a superpower meeting in Reykjavik, even the prospect of a deep cut in nuclear arms. People slept in cardboard boxes in the subways, and there was a cut in social benefits; but there were left-handed mugs, designer Band-Aids and Belgian chocolates in all the boutiques. It was a rather abrasive summer all round, for the North didn't like the South, or the South the North, the poor didn't like the rich, or the rich the poor, and life seemed harsher but cleaner, harder but firmer. It was cold in England, but warmer abroad, which was no bad place to be that season, a season when the world seemed to be changing fast, and things growing very different. And that, more or less, was how it was over that particular summer, the summer of the cuts.

2

In the boardroom on the fortieth floor of the great new glass tower that housed Eldorado Television, high above a great sad northern city, they were cutting steak.

It was the weekly board lunch, and Lord Mellow, the board chairman, sat at the head of the long table, in his familiar bow-tie. Most of the board members, from old Lord Lenticule to the Bishop of Whiddicupthwaite, who was Eldorado's religious advisor, had struggled in, in their chauffeur-driven cars, from their manor houses on the broad acres of the nearby shires, and they sat near their chairman toward the top of the table. Lord Mellow also made it his custom to invite a few of the television executives who happened to be greatly in favour with him that week – because they had made a good programme, or were in the running for a BAFTA award, or were at risk of being poached by some other company rather bigger than Eldorado itself. For Eldorado, for all its great building, was one of the smaller and more remote of the independent programme companies. It was generally considered a great pity that, in the random lottery of the franchise, it should have had to locate its premises and talents in a northern region that seemed to specialise exclusively in rundown mills, tired industrial conurbations with bleak backstreets, dark heathen moorland where strange beasts, animal and human, roamed, and where a general economic gloom prevailed. For this part of the world had, to be frank, not done very well out of the cuts.

All the same, the landscape offered many stories of bleak human truth, set against good grainy locations, and the 600 or so talented people who worked in the Eldorado glass tower all said they enjoyed it, however much it may have been that they preferred to be in London, or better Hollywood, where in their business most of the real and exciting inaction was to be found. And there was much to be said for it; Lord Mellow may have been an intemperate man, but he was a go-ahead, ambitious chairman, and was considered to look after his staff extremely well. The fine new glass building where they sat at the lunch-table was a testimony to his forward-looking instincts. It had been commissioned from a well-known hi-tech architect who was said to have worked with Richard Rogers on the Beaubourg and Norman Foster on the bank in Hong Kong, and certainly, like all the best new buildings that year, it had an atrium in the middle and cranes on the roof. You could work, if you did, in your office thirty floors up, and look out of the window to see technicians waving at you as they rushed by outside. A novel interior designer, a green-haired lady who had just done three London hotels, had turned all sorts of things into high-presentation features no one thought they were, and plastic heating vents, interior plumbing, and naked electric wires had been painted red and highlighted, giving an atmosphere of modern fun to the building. The outside caterers, who wore teeshirts with the word GNOSH on them as they served at table, were as noted for their *nouvelle cuisine* as they were for their *nouveau Beaujolais*; and Lord Mellow kept an excellent cellar, somewhere up there on the fortieth floor. It was always a pleasure to be invited to the Eldorado board lunch.

So, over the big northern city, which hummed away indifferently below, they gathered to eat heartily: the board members, in their big-prowed business suits, all of them old-looking, even when they were not, and the favoured television executives, clad in the studied informalities of their calling, all of them young-looking, even when they were not. To these lunches it was Lord Mellow's practice to ask one special guest – a distinguished figure from the world of politics, business or the arts, who had either had some special connection with Eldorado or else could probably do the company some very significant favour. This week it was Sir Luke Trimingham, the great theatrical knight. Sir Luke had been famous in youth for his exceptional beauty and his way of throwing his long limbs about the stage. Now, in his silver years, he had attained yet more eminence for a declamatory poetic diction so fine that he no longer needed to move about the stage at all.

'In my younger day, now well past,' he was saying, in that manner of slow deliberation only permitted to the most eminent celebrities, 'when I was in my filmic prime ...'

'Do re-fill Sir Luke's glass,' said Lord Mellow, seizing the arm of a man from GNOSH. It was well-known that this was quite the best way to release Sir Luke's inexhaustible capacity for reminiscence.

'Bless you, dear boy,' said Sir Luke, beaming. 'Yes, in my heyday, when an experienced director wished to depict a couple making love, he always cut away to a field of waving corn. That was the convention. How things have changed. Now, when an experienced director wishes to depict a field of waving corn, what does he do?'

12

'He cuts away to a couple making love?' suggested Lord Mellow, renowned in the building for being famously quick on the uptake.

'It was my line, dear boy, but have it if you must,' said Sir Luke. 'That is what I call a change without an improvement. We must bring in sex here, brutal violence there, anything to stimulate the jaded palates of our audiences. In our living rooms we can watch the world's parade of vain and pointless egos, the random display of the most obscene and perverted desires. I know, you young people will say the boring old fart has grown stuffy in his failing years ...'

'Not at all,' said all the board and some of the executives, most of whom had, over time, grown practised in the art of showing great tolerance to the famous.

'Taste, discretion, subtlety, art,' said Sir Luke. 'For me those things have always gone together. Ah, where are the cutaways of yesteryear, *ou sont les coups d'antan?*'

'Things have changed,' said Lord Mellow. 'The stakes are high, and getting higher every minute.' One of the men from GNOSH peered anxiously over his shoulder.

'I had always understood that British film and television drama led the field,' said Sir Luke, seizing the man from GNOSH and having him fill his glass again. 'We may be sinking giggling into the sea, but none can bow to us, surely, in the matter of filmic quality.'

'That was true, a few years back,' said Lord Mellow. 'Our work was just like a Fortnum and Mason's fruitcake. You couldn't beat it for weight and taste and quality.'

'We had the entire world wanting to revisit Brideshead,' said Sir Luke. 'And *The Jewel in the Crown* was definitely a jewel in our crown.'

13

'And that was the problem,' said Lord Mellow. 'I know quality when I see it, and those boys probably didn't know the harm they were doing.'

'What was that?' asked Sir Luke.

'They just priced quality right off the market,' said Lord Mellow. 'Do you have any idea what those big series cost?'

'Oh, money, money,' said Sir Luke. 'I have never understood it. I let my agent person think about that.'

'It's ruined the profession,' said Lord Mellow. 'The secretarial temps all come in now and talk about high production values. Every trainee cameraman expects a six-month shoot in India on triple pay before he can pull a focus. We've got young directors now who can't begin to shoot a scene unless they're up above it in a helicopter. It's destroying the small companies like Eldorado. In this building we have to cut our coats according to our cloth.'

'I must say this is a most benign concoction,' said Sir Luke, summoning over the man from GNOSH. 'What is it? An Aloxe-Corton, I fancy. Do slip a bottle or two into the pocket of my Burberry.'

'I like quality,' said Lord Mellow. 'I said so at the Edinburgh Festival and now I'm stuck with it. I like quality, but I like it cheap. And available to everyone.'

'"According to the fair play of the world,/ Let me have audience,"' said Sir Luke. 'That, I take it, is what you mean?'

'Just what I mean,' said Lord Mellow.

'I feared as much,' said Sir Luke. 'Well, I have seen some of your dramatic work. The ubiquitous videotape, which I have always thought fit only for home movies. That special brand of actor who has learned the sum of his trade making voice-overs for commercials. Those endless studio sets where you fight the Battle of Waterloo with three people on each side. That charming little touch of always having the microphone boom just peeping in at the top of the picture. Yes, I know your work.'

'Fill Sir Luke's glass again,' said Lord Mellow to the man from GNOSH, and he turned back to his guest. 'Now this is just what I wanted to talk to you about. We've been thinking about a really high-quality drama with a really bankable star.'

'Are you sure this is wise?' said Sir Luke. 'There are cuts everywhere, you know.'

'The streets are choking with money if you know how to get it,' said Lord Mellow.

'Are they really?' said Sir Luke. 'I can't say I understand such matters.'

'If we had a really bankable star we could get worldwide co-production money,' said Lord Mellow. 'And prime time on the major American networks.'

'This hardly sounds like Eldorado,' said Sir Luke.

'Ah,' said Lord Mellow. 'You may not know this, but our franchise comes up for renewal quite soon. And we've been given a very heavy hint we may not get it again unless we do some high-quality drama.'

'Really?' said Sir Luke. 'I do play golf a good deal with the top people at the IBA, but I don't recall they ever mentioned this to me.'

'I think the moment has come to try for the peaks,' said Lord Mellow. 'And this is why we sent that script to you. You probably haven't had time to read it.'

'Oh yes,' said Sir Luke. 'I read it in the back of the car on the way up to this delightful repast.'

'Fill Sir Luke's glass again,' said Lord Mellow to the

man from GNOSH.

'Mellow, may I tell you something?' said Sir Luke. 'I am quite an old man now, sound in wind and limb, fit in all appurtenances, but not exactly young. I have set myself two strict rules for my senior years. One is never to appear nude in any filmic drama. The other is never to be seen playing the ukelele.'

'Very natural,' said Lord Mellow. 'But what did you think of the script?'

'Mellow, that script requires I do both,' said Sir Luke. 'I am neither a flasher nor a song and dance man. I think you confused me with Sir Laurence.'

'I don't believe it,' said Lord Mellow, staring down the table at the television executives, who, mostly congregated at the lower end, were sharing the last of the parsnips. 'What, *Gladstone, Man of Empire?*'

'I assure you, Mellow,' said Sir Luke. 'Oh, the writing is totally incompetent and by someone very famous on an off-day, but that I expect and can tolerate. The parts are without exception quite unplayable and the lines unspeakable, but believe me, I do not insist on fine lines or sound motivations, 'twere folly to do so. I have long been known for the ability to give meaning to roles totally devoid of sense. That is what acting is about.'

'Fill Sir Luke's glass again,' said Lord Mellow to the man from GNOSH. 'So you have a few criticisms of the script?'

'I simply find it hard to believe that Mr Gladstone ever appeared in the nude before Queen Victoria at Windsor,' said Sir Luke. 'And even more unlikely that he did so while playing the ukelele.'

'Is this true, Pride?' asked Lord Mellow, looking again down the table.

'The script's by one of the best in the business,' said Jocelyn Pride, a tousle-headed youth of middle years who was Head of Drama Plays and Series at Eldorado.

'I have no doubt of it at all,' said Sir Luke. 'He is undoubtedly a most prestigious name, as are those of so many untalented people who surround us these days.'

'All of us in drama have totally rewritten and edited it,' said Cynthia Hyde-Lemon, a very big girl in a yellow jumpsuit, who was Head of Productions.

'I have no doubt of that either,' said Sir Luke. 'Nobody who has access to a manuscript would dream of leaving it alone.'

'Gladstone and the ukelele,' said Lord Mellow.

'Ah, well, this is a drama-doc,' said Jocelyn Pride. 'It's fictionalised verity. You take real people and events but you're not slavishly bound to actual facts.'

'I see,' said Sir Luke. 'So this is a form of fictional licence. Do explain it to me I'm awfully dull, you know.'

'We're trying to turn boring old facts into visual symbolic images,' said Jocelyn Pride. 'We want to convey the inner meaning of the story, semiotically. You see, television is a very visual medium.'

'Ah,' said Sir Luke. 'And this explains why people sit in front of screens and watch it?'

'Quite,' said Pride. 'And this writer is world-famous for his surreal motifs.'

'So was the author of *The 120 Days of Sodom*,' said Sir Luke. 'I suppose you will soon be offering me a part in that?'

'Fill Sir Luke's glass again,' said Lord Mellow decisively, before Pride could reply. 'We costume you in frock coats right the way through. We strike the ukelele.'

'Dear boy', said Sir Luke, tossing back his head, 'I am

an actor. Naturally I like to work. I have consented to play in dramas of the most incredible absurdity. I have permitted myself to play opposite madmen and nympho-maniacs who have practised their vile trade on the set before my eyes, not to say those of the entire public. I have done many things. I have even worked in religious broadcasting.'

'It's amazing,' said Lord Mellow.

'And, Mellow, I assure you,' said Sir Luke, 'nothing would please me more than to play the part of Mr Gladstone. It's one I've long coveted. But as far as this script is concerned, I can only say what the great man would doubtless say himself were he here. It is definitely not my bag.'

'I see,' said Lord Mellow, thinking hard.

'That script is worthy neither of me nor you,' said Sir Luke. 'Take my advice, the advice of one of the oldest and most experienced old bores in the business. You will not get the franchise with this. To my mind it would afford good grounds for banning the lot of you from practising in television again for life.'

'This is very worrying,' said Lord Mellow. 'We've been developing that story for the last two years. Seven Oxford historians did the research. Fifty talented people rewrote the script five times.'

'Of course you could say I'm growing very stuffy and pompous in my late years,' said Sir Luke.

The board members and the television executives sat around the table in front of their long-empty plates, and said nothing.

'Supposing we were able to find you a really first-class vehicle ...' Lord Mellow finally murmured.

'Would I be prepared to travel in it?' said Sir Luke. 'I'm

glad you mentioned that. Could you have someone call my own? The driver is about somewhere. And I have to fly to Las Vegas tomorrow. I'm doing a tap-dance number with Barbra Streisand.'

Sir Luke rose to his feet and the man from GNOSH helped the great knight on with his coat, which clanked noisily. The television executives and the members of the board rose too, save for old Lord Lenticule, whom the meal had clearly exhausted.

'Would you?' asked Lord Mellow, walking his guest down the long room. 'If all these brilliant and talented people I hire could come up with the ideal series?'

'I might, I just possibly might,' said the great knight. 'Provided, only provided, that it not be that one, or anything like it.'

'See me in the penthouse suite right away,' murmured Lord Mellow to Jocelyn Pride as he passed him. The two senior figures made their way out on to the landing, overlooking the atrium. A glass lift could be seen travelling toward them up the great inner wall of the building. As they waited, Sir Luke tore a notice off a nearby notice-board and wrote something on the back of it.

'I enjoyed our repast,' said Sir Luke. 'I wish I could say the same of the script. Oh, here is a note of my expenses. I had thought you a good deal nearer to London.'

'So had we,' said Lord Mellow, looking at the note. 'Well, I do hope we'll have the chance of working together.'

'You had better discuss that with my agent,' said Sir Luke. 'Or my agent's agent. As you rightly said, I am remarkably bankable.' The glass lift reached the landing and three people got out, all of them looking down with a hideous apprehension at the great well up which they had travelled. But Sir Luke got in as into the glow of a great spotlight, his pockets clanking noisily.

'Ah, what a shot this would make!' he cried, pressing the button. 'One could take it from just across there!'

'Quite,' murmured Lord Mellow. 'If one had brought one's shotgun.' And he hurried back toward the penthouse suite.

3

In the penthouse suite, even before Lord Mellow returned, they were already cutting their losses.

On the fortieth floor of the great glass tower that was Eldorado, Lord Mellow had reserved a large area for himself. There was his vast office, with three secretaries, a white desk and several large Danish settees, into which his guests and employees sank as if into a foam bath. There was his reception room, stocked with fine wines and extraordinary liqueurs, mysterious Stregas and plum brandies from the Tatra Mountains, in which if all had gone well the pre- and post- production parties for the various Eldorado projects were held. Beyond that, on the other side of great glass doors, there was his huge white bedroom, with seven television screens hung over the vast fourposter vibrator bed, and even further beyond that his marble bathroom, with double whirly-bath, ceiling mirrors, and more television receivers – for Lord Mellow liked to know everything that was going on in the building, even when he was at stool. The Eldorado empire was large, and contained many things – amusement arcades and motorway service stations, a patio furniture company and a satellite corporation, an oil-rig or two in the North Sea and a mine that mined something antipodean or other in Australia. But television was Lord Mellow's first love, and he lived and slept Eldorado, ate and drank it, bathed, showered and changed it. There was a Lady Mellow, but she was used only for special public occasions in London, and had

21

never been known to travel north. Lord Mellow was here all the time, when he was not somewhere abroad, juggling money or inventing new projects or international conglomerates. He woke in his bed the moment the first transmissions started, watching the screens and already beginning to summon staff to him over breakfast with peremptory messages. He raged and flattered and shouted and wept all through the day, until transmissions ceased in the early hours, when he fell, often fully clothed, into his vast bed, while the seven screens still beamed out satellite pictures from the great media globe that was his oyster.

'Jesus, Joss,' said Cynthia Hyde-Lemon, the Head of Productions. 'What made you send that load of junk to that silly old bugger? You know he's as thick as thieves with old Mellow.'

'I don't know who sent it to him,' said Jocelyn Pride, who of course did.

Three or four members of the board who did not have to fly to Hong Kong right away or take an afternoon nap sat in the Danish settees and looked at him unsympathetically. So did several of the television executives: there were four men with blowdry haircuts and heavy tans, who were head of this and that and the other; there was Cynthia Hyde-Lemon, big in her yellow jumpsuit, and there was an even bigger girl in calf-length cardigan and kneewarmers whom no one seemed to recognise. Jocelyn Pride was a whizz-kid of forty who had developed the Eldorado drama policy, a cunning construct by which plodding and deeply conventional scripts hurriedly written by half-experienced authors were cheaply shot, with, however, actors of world fame. He wore brown suits and suede shoes, a taste ill-received in the office but assumed to go down very well in Hollywood, where he seemed to spend most of his time. Here he constructed extraordinary co-production deals and made arrangements for international casting, so that American movie stars of enormous reputation suddenly appeared in Eldorado productions, playing cockney waiters, north country farm labourers, eminent dowagers and British members of Parliament with a fine indifference to any laws of verisimilitude, but with excellent results in world-wide residual sales. Nobody liked Pride, not least for his suede shoes, but he was known to have a brilliant touch, and it was hard to believe now that he was losing it.

'Who's going to carry the can?' asked the Head of Finance, who was acting as portboy, and was going round the room with a decanter, coffee and after-dinner mints. 'He'll be in one of his raging tempers.'

'I never read the scripts properly,' said Cynthia Hyde-Lemon. 'And I never really liked the idea anyway. Whose was it?'

'It was his,' said Joss Pride, bitterly. 'But we can't tell him that. Look, we're all in this together.'

'Right,' said Lord Mellow, coming in, sitting down heavily at his big white desk, and looking round the group. 'Who's going to jump out of the window first? I want someone to jump out of that window and stain the pavement. I don't care who, but I want it right away.'

'Evidently some error has occurred,' said Lord Lenticule, the oldest board member. 'I say no more than that.'

'I'll say an error has occurred,' said Lord Mellow. 'I spent half a million getting that script developed.'

'Lord Mellow,' said Jocelyn Pride, 'we did actually

23

discuss it in detail with you.'

'You thought it had everything,' said Cynthia Hyde-Lemon, in her big yellow jumpsuit.

'Great country houses, royals, political conflict, the Irish question, lots of Empire,' said Jocelyn Pride.

'Beautiful locations, India, the Crimea ...' said a man in a bow-tie: the Head of Technical Staff.

'Ireland, the Balkans,' added Jocelyn Pride.

'Liverpool for grim actuality,' put in Cynthia Hyde-Lemon.

'And a fucking ukelele,' said Lord Mellow. 'Nobody talked ukeleles to me.'

'It was a late development,' said Pride.

'Look, it's not essential we have old Luke Trimingham in it at all,' said Cynthia Hyde-Lemon. 'That was just notional casting.'

Lord Mellow sat at his desk and stared bitterly at them all.

'Sir Luke was right,' he said. 'What I want to know is, who commissioned this garbage? Who thought of bloody Gladstone?'

'I suppose I did,' said Jocelyn Pride, incautiously. 'When you said you wanted a story about a nineteenth-century British prime minister who was interested in prostitutes and the Irish question.'

'I never liked it,' said Lord Mellow. 'I never wanted it. Now I want that script shredded. I want it pulped. I want the waste paper sold abroad. And if you can get the author stuffed bum-down in the shredder as well, that would be a first-rate bonus.'

'Yesterday you said you liked the script,' said Cynthia.

'I was lying, to save you pain,' said Lord Mellow.

'So what do you want, Lord Mellow?' asked Cynthia.

Lord Mellow looked at her, slowly took of his jacket, then spoke very deliberately. 'Cynthia, I do not want Gladstone,' he said. 'I'm through with history. I never want to see another drama about a prime minister screwing his way to the top. I refuse to look at one more shot of that bloody black property door with the number 10 painted on it. I never never never want to see another mockup of the House of Common built in our studio space again. Clear?'

'Clear,' said Cynthia.

'What I want is something international and of this moment,' he said. 'With love and joy in it, along with a little pain. So let's all start thinking, really thinking all over again.'

There was a silence.

'Well, what other scripts have we got in the pile, Joss?' asked Cynthia Hyde-Lemon, fingering the zip of her yellow jumpsuit.

'There's that story about the decline of a great country house, Cyn,' said Pride. 'That's thirteen episodes, the dialogue bounces like a tennis ball, and everyone's into nostalgia now.'

'No,' said Lord Mellow.

'No?' said Jocelyn Pride.

'No, I do not want another big country house with a fucking fountain,' said Lord Mellow. 'I never again wish to see another hero mooning round a Hawksmoor façade twitching his mouth beautifully because no one's written him a single damned line to say. I want a here-and-now story of contemporary actuality. With a strong resourceful hero with lines that anyone can identify and sympathise with.'

'I think we just got a story in about the fall of

Singapore,' said the other big girl, who was not Head of anything, but who had smiled at Lord Mellow in the corridor the previous week.

'I do not want any more End of Empire,' said Lord Mellow. 'Is that all anyone thinks about? I don't want any story where the hero has an arm off. I don't want anything located in any country that gives us a diarrhoea problem. Everyone sits in the boghouse right the way through the shoot, and we never come in on time or budget.'

'There's a story on file about unemployment in Newcastle,' said Jocelyn Pride.

'I don't want it,' said Lord Mellow. 'I don't want Newcastle or anything depressing. I want it strong and I want it dramatic.'

'There's a very good story about marriage break-up,' said Cynthia. 'Set in Hampstead.'

'I don't want it,' said Lord Mellow. 'I want something big and something epic. I want it all on film and I want it shot in elegant locations.'

'But what else is there?' said Jocelyn Pride. 'I mean, we've covered everything that English writers ever write about.'

'Then find new writers,' said Lord Mellow, taking off his braces. 'Forget about your Pinters and Potters and Platers. Find me someone new and original. Who delivers scripts on time and isn't off on a yacht with Bertolucci when you need him for rewrites. Someone who has epic sweep but doesn't think that means writing in millions of pounds on doing the whole of the Retreat from Moscow. Someone who thinks big and strong, but understands the financial costs a series has to work in at Eldorado. Clear?'

'Clear,' said Cynthia.

'I want something that's art, but is also life at its deepest and most telling,' said Lord Mellow, warming to his theme and taking off his shirt. 'I want Mark Hasper to direct and I want to feel his artistic imprint all over it. I want David Hockney titles and George Fenton music. Something visual, luminous, conceptual.'

'It sounds very expensive,' said the Head of Finance.

'On this one we are really not talking chicken-feed,' said Lord Mellow. 'The franchise is up for renewal. The City's full of floating money that's begging to invest in the right-quality artistic package. I don't think I've ever seen so much money on the street looking for the right product. No one else has got a really big one on the stocks so we're certain of prime-time scheduling. We don't have to be mean with this one.'

'So are we talking four to six?' asked Cynthia.

'I'm thinking more ten to thirteen,' said Lord Mellow.

'An original or an adaptation?' asked Jocelyn Pride.

'I'm talking an original,' said Lord Mellow. 'A brand-new story that has the real aroma of success. And with the talent that surrounds me here I know we can find it.'

'We'll have to go out and commission,' said Cynthia. 'There's nothing in at all like that at the moment.'

'Go and commission,' said Lord Mellow. 'Find a new writer who writes like a dream in a prestigious way. *And* creates parts Brando would work for nothing to get. Is it quite clear now what I want?'

'Very clear,' said Cynthia. 'An unknown with a mind of a genius would do. But it won't be easy.'

'We don't work in television because it's easy,' said Lord Mellow. 'We work here because we like to fly by the seat of our knickers. Because we thrive on challenge and opportunity. Now – go and get thriving on it.'

Lord Mellow took off his trousers and stood in his underpants. For most of the staff, except for his trustworthy secretaries, this was generally taken as a signal to leave. Lord Mellow was always changing to get on to his next appointment, or so it was thought. So the executives put down their port glasses, rose from the Danish settees, woke Lord Lenticule, and headed for the corridor.

'And I want it shot in the autumn and shown in the spring,' shouted Lord Mellow after them.

Out on the landing, as they waited for the lift to come, they stared at each other. In the circumstances, Lord Mellow had been quite temperate.

Nobody talked to Jocelyn Pride. He wore awful brown suits and ridiculous suede shoes. He was never here and, when he was, was aloof with his staff. He had not had a BAFTA award for any of his productions for years. His spectacles looked wrong. Perhaps the whizz-kid wasn't whizzing any more.

'Shoot in the autumn!' said the Head of Finance.

'He didn't say he wanted it cheap,' said Cynthia.

'And I want it cheap,' said Lord Mellow, standing in the door of his suite, a large fleshy shape, clad only in his socks and supporting suspenders.

'You see now why we wrote in the ukelele,' said Cynthia to the Head of Technical Staff.

4

In the tiny and depressing hill-village where Henry Babbacombe, an author virtually unknown, even to himself, lived and breathed and had his being, they were cutting the corn.

Great gantry-like machines, high-powered combine harvesters with great front teeth, stereo in the cab, central locking and racing stripes were thundering through the nearby fields, shaking the soil, shuddering the trees, and rocking the foundations, if there were some, of the small and gloomy garden shed amid the weeds at the bottom of Henry's cottage garden, beside the graveyard, where he sat and wrote his books. Very small harvest mites – the people down in the village, secretive, remote people whom Henry rarely saw, except when peering out through windows, called them 'thunderbugs' – filled the air in great black clouds. Even in the garden shed there was absolutely no refuge from them. They crowded into Henry's hair, his eyes, his nose, and into those of the girl from Radio Haywain, the local independent radio station, whose tape recorder Henry had, after long effort, just managed to get working.

'I don't understand these things, not properly,' said the girl from Radio Haywain. 'I'm not a real reporter, I just work for them on an MSC scheme. Radio Haywain's a very small but enterprising station.'

'I think it should work quite well now,' said Henry Babbacombe. 'If you just keep an eye on this little gauge just here. I'm sorry I can't do any better than that, but

29

I'm not used to being interviewed.'

'This one here?' said the girl. 'All right, now, Mr Babbacombe, first could you tell me what you had for breakfast?'

'For breakfast?' said Henry, who, although, as he constantly told himself, he had published three important books and was surely on the edge of a great breakthrough in his career, had indeed never been interviewed. 'Ah, well, I ate my usual diet of high fibre cereal, with decaffeinated coffee. And after that I wrote down my dreams.'

'Your dreams?' said the girl from Radio Haywain.

'Dreams and writing are extremely closely related, as science has proved,' said Henry Babbacombe confidently.

'I didn't know that,' said the girl, peering at the voice level gauge. 'I'm just on an MSC scheme. I'll switch it on now.'

'I thought you already had,' said Henry. 'I thought we'd started.'

'That was for level,' said the girl. 'Can you just show me where to start it going?'

Henry showed her. The girl smiled and pushed a microphone under his nose.

'Today I'm with Mr Henry Babbacombe of Smallby, who is well-known for having written three quite well-known novels,' she began. 'Mr Babbacombe, I'm sitting with you in a small old shed at the bottom of your garden. Is this where you do all your writing?'

'Yes, it is,' said Henry. 'I always work out here in this garden shed on an old Remington Portable. My work habits are very simple. I rise at eight, after sleeping well. I eat my breakfast ...'

'Someone told me you eat high fibre cereal,' said the girl.

'Exactly, and I write down my dreams. Then I run a mile, and sit down to work. I always keep regular hours. Even if you have nothing to say, you should always write. If young writers ask me, I always tell them that. At six I stop and prepare a simple salad.'

'You just sit here all day in this old shed and write?' asked the girl. 'That's all you do?'

'More or less,' said Henry Babbacombe.

'Don't you ever feel cut off?' said the girl. 'Oh, oh, oh, Mr Babbacombe, just then I felt the earth move.'

'Yes,' said Henry. The earth had indeed moved, and they waited for a moment or two until the combine had moved off toward the other end of the field.

'No, it's the ideal place for me to commune with my thoughts,' said Henry, 'Writing is mostly thinking, I find.'

'So you do a lot of thinking, Mr Babbacombe,' said the girl. 'And is there anything special you do to get inspired?'

'Well, I whistle a lot,' said Henry. 'My tastes are classical.'

'I see, so you sit there and wait for an idea to come. How do you know when you've got one?' asked the girl.

'I always say ideas are like colours,' said Henry. 'The book I'm writing now is yellow, vivid yellow. Everywhere in it I try to keep this yellow feeling.'

'But what's it about?'

'About? I'm not sure there's an about about for a book to be actually *about*, are you?' asked Henry. 'I'm afraid I doubt the existence of an external reality.'

'I can see how you would, sitting here all day on your

tod in an old shed like this,' said the girl. 'But wouldn't you say the writer has a responsibility, I mean, with all the unemployment, and the deprivation, and the cuts, and the computer revolution, I mean, doesn't that worry you, don't you feel you ought to write about that?'

'Naturally as a maker of fictions I believe the world is a fiction,' said Henry. 'I am competing with the world, not trying vulgarly to imitate it.'

'Well, I've not actually read one of your books, I'm only on an MSC scheme, but could you give our listeners an idea what they're like? Apart from being yellow? I mean, tell us the titles.'

'The first is called *Numen*, the second *Composition 2* and the third *Composition 4*. There was one in between that was never published,' said Henry.

'Oh, yes,' said the girl. 'And could you compare them to *Watership Down*, for instance?'

'Ah, my influences,' said Henry. 'I'd say my work falls somewhere roughly between Eco and Endo.'

'Oh, yes?' said the girl.

'It displays the semiotic preoccupation of the former and the formal exactitude and precise imagery of the latter.'

'Are these two local?' asked the girl. 'You know this is a local station.'

'One is Italian, one is Japanese,' said Henry contemptuously. 'We live in a desert without an oasis and we must summon our refreshment from afar.'

'They said in the village you lecture at the university,' said the girl from the MSC scheme, looking desperate.

'I am a lecturer, in the department of Extra-Mural Studies,' said Henry.

'Like it?' said the girl.

'I always say it's an ideal place for an outsider to be,' said Henry with an urbane laugh.

'But look, if you've got a job, how can you spend so much time stuck here in this shed?'

'Because in adult education you lecture in the evenings. This gives me quite a long writing day, an ideal arrangement for a creator.'

'So you write all day and then you teach in the evenings,' said the girl. 'I imagine you're not married, then?'

'No, I'm not,' said Henry. 'Somehow I've never seemed to meet the right person.'

'You wouldn't, would you?' said the girl from the MSC. 'Unless someone fell out of an aeroplane and landed in the shed. Well, Henry Babbacombe, writer extraordinary, thank you very much. How does this machine go off?'

'You will let me know when it's going out, won't you?' said Henry Babbacombe anxiously, after he had stopped the tape recorder. 'I never have time to listen to radio normally.'

'I will, if they put it out,' said the girl.

'Why wouldn't they?' asked Henry.

'Well,' said the girl, 'I wouldn't really know. I told you, I'm only on an MSC scheme. Perhaps all that noise outside. Incidentally I think you've got a rat in your wastepaper basket.'

'It's just the field-mice,' said Henry. 'They always come and shelter inside when they're cutting the barley.'

The door of the shed opened, and a flood of harvest mites and Mrs Raper from the village, who, as she said, did for Henry, came in.

'Oh, Mr Babbacombe, that phone of yours has been

ringing and ringing,' said Mrs Raper. 'Someone from Eldorado TV wants you very urgent. They been trying to reach you these past two days. They was beginning to think you'd cut yourself right off.'

'Not at all,' said Henry, rising from the wooden milking stool on which he worked. 'Eldorado Television? I expect that's another interview. I'll come at once.'

'Don't forget to tell them all about that old yellow feeling,' said the girl from Radio Haywain, roping in the lead of her tape recorder, which for some reason appeared not to be connected to anything in the wall at all. 'And thanks a million.'

5

In the back of a vast grey Ford Granada, sitting in acrylic comfort behind a grey-uniformed, black-capped chauffeur as the car drove smoothly through the big northern city where Eldorado held its fiefdom, Henry Babbacombe could not but feel that he was cutting something of a dash.

For a long-ignored writer there was something very grand about gliding through the crowded buzzing streets of a great city, holding on to a strap, leaning back on a padded headrest, surveying the world through the glass. The streets were filled with noisy youthful people who constantly threw beercans at each other, and were quite different from those of the various small market towns where, in tiny wooden branch libraries in the late evenings, when almost everyone else was asleep, he taught his evening classes on 'Sex and Maturity in the English Novel' and the rather more popular 'Fiction and the Farm'. That was the world he was used to; the world in which his creativity flourished.

Probably it had been a mistake to leave it, on what looked like an increasingly futile venture. But Mr Jocelyn Pride, who had called him on the telephone from Eldorado Television, had been really most pressing about his making this visit. Words had been spoken down the wire about his prodigious and versatile talent that had been very gratifying. It was true that Mr Pride showed no signs of familiarity with the novels he so warmly praised, but like every writer, and every human being, Henry liked to be liked, and he quite took to Mr Pride. Even so he had been cautious, carefully explaining that, because he taught at night, and in any case much preferred writing his own writing to sitting there watching the writing other people had written, he had never bothered to acquire a television box, though he did watch his mother's when he went home at Christmas. Even this obvious impediment had not deterred Mr Pride. 'Great, that means you're not tainted,' he had cried, and this at least was certainly true. He issued an imperious summons for Henry to come right over to Eldorado the next day.

But when he put down the phone, Henry realised that he had absolutely no idea just why the summons had come. Perhaps it was for a studio interview about *Composition 4*, which had certainly not had the attention it deserved. Perhaps it was for something more in-depth, like a tramp through the landscape of his childhood, in the council housing estate in Grimsby, where he had first conceived his love of abstract art. Well, he would be cautious; the one thing a great writer must always keep is his integrity. The following morning, when he rose to make the trip, the idea had become even less attractive. Though the great glass tower of Eldorado and the small garden shed where Henry worked were both in the north of England, the north is a rather vaster place than is sometimes thought by people in the south, or indeed by Henry himself, and the pieces of it do not connect together with any ease at all. To reach Eldorado by twelve, Henry had to rise at five – not of itself a difficult matter, since the combine harvesters had continued to thunder right through the night, making the floor of his bedroom shudder, casting great searchlight beams into its deepest recesses and making sleep impossible. He had to shorten his jog, then get into his car and drive twenty miles over roads of deplorable quality to the nearest railway station, for in some long-past era of cuts the once-excellent railway services had been more or less stripped from the region. Henry's car was an ancient Morris Traveller, which he had purchased for its vaguely wattle-and-daub construction. Alas, like most people who purchase medieval estates, he had not reckoned with the heavy wind and cold airs that habitually pass through them. Ripe smells of cowdung filled the vehicle, the high fibre cereal sat heavy in his stomach and a cold Siberian mistral battered the vehicle as it passed over the moorland tops. Even worse, once he reached the railway Henry knew he would have to put up with the world.

The world was worse than he thought. The diesel pay-train that took him on the next step of his travels rattled through moorland on a distorted and crumbling track that made the marking of the pile of essays on *Middlemarch* he had brought with him to delight his journey next to impossible. Then the coach had filled with fumes from the train exhaust, causing the guard to position himself permanently next to the fire extinguisher, and covering Henry with a thick glaze of grease. When he reached the grim urban complex, consisting largely of abandoned colliery headstocks and weed-grown railway yards, where he had to change to a larger train, Henry was already despairing of the trip. In the great express from London, tugged by an exhausted diesel locomotive, Henry now found himself surrounded by young people wearing strange headsets which apparently allowed them to listen to their own insides. Beyond the window was an extraordinary landscape: from high stone viaducts overarching grey industrial cities, he looked down on vast factories that were being dismantled or demolished, old mills from the great age of wool and cotton that were collapsing into polluted rivers, great postwar housing estates where all the buildings had been boarded up. Style-artists had spray-painted every para-pet and abutment with highly colourful obscenities which were probably the hostile names of pop groups. On every platform where the train halted, there were strange wild bands of people: young female witches entirely dressed in black, their faces powdered white with black rings round the eyes, chains about their waists and ankles; weird mutilated youths, bald save for great cockscombs of orange hair, and chests let out to strange advertisers; old ladies in tracksuits, old men with tee-shirts saying 'Screw me'; innumerable Princess Di lookalikes; tonsured members of unusual sects with begging bowls. As the girl from Radio Haywain had suggested to him, very odd things were happening in the world of the cuts.

There were moments when Henry was glad he was a writer, for writers could live in their own minds and didn't have to go outside at all. Yet perhaps there were compensations. For, when he reached the terminus and walked down the platform, there was a man in uniform holding up a sign with *Mr Henry Babbacombe* written on it in the largest of letters, and he saw that in a world where everyone was hungry for recognition he at least had some. The driver had led him off to the Ford Granada, and now he sat there, a drinks cabinet like an old cinema organ in front of him, the strange world safely on the other side of the glass. It was certainly a very mixed and funny sort of world, the modern world of today, and probably quite engrossing if you could find a way of writing about it, without getting too involved in reality, which of course did not exist anyway.

Up in front, the chauffeur, sitting there in his black hat and grey uniform, coughed respectfully and turned to look at Henry.

'Mind if I cut up here through the back streets and avoid all this traffic, sir?' he said. 'Lord Mellow always likes me to do that.'

'Certainly, go the best way you know,' said Henry, stretching his legs.

'Of course I'm really Lord Mellow's chauffeur, sir,' said the driver, 'but he's using the helicopter today. He's off to London for the BAFTA awards. I believe he's seeing you first. Fascinating man, Lord Mellow.'

'Really?' said Henry. 'Who actually is he?'

'I take it you're not in the television business yourself then, sir,' said the chauffeur.

'Not yet,' said Henry.

'Perhaps you're from an eastern country, or something?' asked the chauffeur.

'Not exactly,' said Henry, 'but from pretty far away.'

'Well, Lord Mellow's chairman of the board and the associated companies, sir,' said the chauffeur.

'Is he really?' said Henry.

'I get all kinds in here, you know, sir,' said the driver. 'Celebrities. I had Joan Collins and Prince Andrew in the back last week – not together, naturally. David Puttnam, Steven Spielberg, I've seen them all.'

'Have you really?' said Henry.

'And yourself, sir?' asked the driver.

'I'm a writer,' said Henry.

'I see, sir,' said the chauffeur, and for some reason he said no more after that until they arrived at the great glass tower of Eldorado Television, which rose high above the skyline and shone in the midday sun.

'Go straight in to reception,' said the driver. 'They're expecting you.' And Henry went into a tropical-plant-filled foyer where a fountain rippled and a security man felt him under the arms and then between the legs, and looked into his briefcase. Then a receptionist of Chinese extraction asked him who he was for and who he was, recognised his name on a list, rang a number and scribbled out a security pass.

'Plin to your lapel,' she said. 'Mr Plide's office is on floor ten, Mr Babbacombe. Use the lift over there and Mr Plide's secretary meet you. Thank you, Mr Babbacombe.'

Henry showed his lapel to another security man and went and stood in the great glass lift. High above him soared the great atrium of Eldorado, plants in profusion greening its interior walls. Three blondes with clipboards and a man in glasses got in. 'Underwear, knickers, corsets and bras,' said the man as the lift began to climb the side of the atrium, and the blondes laughed. Henry thought he recognised the man, from his mother's television set, as a northern comedian of some fame, though he looked different in his glasses. 'Vibrators, rubber dolls, dildos, filthy magazines, Terry Wogan,' said the comedian at the next floor, and the blondes laughed a good deal. Henry got out, and looked back. It was all so different, so much more exciting, in this new world of the media, and not at all like teaching evening classes to old ladies in little branch libraries, even though once you got to know it well it would probably seem just a bit superficial.

Then Henry was met by a secretary and taken to the waiting room of Mr Pride's office. Four big actors were sitting there waiting to do read-throughs for a role where the one who got the part would have to fall off a high rooftop and die, and they tried out dying on one another until a door opened and they were called inside. A writer came in with some scripts, and was told to go away and never come back. A man in motor-cycle gear with FILM EXPRESS on his back came in with a round metal tin which he said held rushes from Egypt, though it did not look like it. The secretary offered him coffee and when he asked for his usual decaffeinated she did not mind at all. Then a door opened and a tousle-headed man in a brown suit came out and shook him warmly by the hand, explaining he was Jocelyn Pride. He took Henry inside a very comfortable room with many sofas and there was a very handsomely substantial lady in a black jumpsuit, called Cynthia Hyde-Lemon, who said, 'Good-oh, I want my lunch.'

It was when they went to lunch at an elegantly restored firehouse somewhere in the commercial heart of the city that Henry began to wonder whether he had really been asked here to do an interview about his book at all. Jocelyn and Cynthia talked about it a good deal, and made it clear they had loved it almost to distraction; Henry looked down at the venison and gorgonzola pâté with kiwi fruit in front of him, laid out so beautifully it was a pity to disturb it, as indeed it proved, and beamed with pleasure. Jocelyn and Cynthia raised their Buck's Fizzes to him, and he sensed larger purposes in view. Perhaps they would ask him to adapt his novel as a series? If so, he would certainly stick out for it to be done in colour. And he would be sure to maintain his integrity, because integrity was all a great writer had.

'Well, let's talk television,' said Joss, over the blood-red rack of lamb with kiwi fruit, and then he and Cyn began discussing some vast new drama project Eldorado was undertaking. Joss took out a coffee-stained envelope with some notes on the back of it and began explaining the idea, which did not seem entirely consistent. He spoke of contemporary reality, strong hero, elegant locations. He said artistic, realistic, visual, luminous, conceptual. He said something about shot in the autumn and shown in the spring. It was not until the kiwi fruit sorbet arrived that Henry realised that they were asking him if he would write it.

'Me?' he asked.

'We've listened to you, Henry,' said Cyn. 'And we like you, Henry.'

It seemed an absurdly large project, as Henry thought about it, but as they sat there for another hour and drank three bottles of a Leoville-Barton red wine someone had mentioned was very good, Henry began to feel that he had more or less got it worked out.

'I see it as essentially puce,' he said.

'Excellent,' said Cynthia Hyde-Lemon.

'And set in an unknown foreign country which is not quite reality,' said Henry. 'You see in reality I don't really believe in reality.'

'You're right,' said Cynthia, pointing a finger at him. 'You're utterly, completely right. People talk about weality as if we could joint the camera, point the camera, right at it and that's it. As Roland Barthes – wasn't it Woland Barthes? – said, weality is simply a semiotic construct.'

'Barthes, or possibly Eco,' said Henry, feeling he was with his own kind of people at last. 'Actually I'm very much influenced by Eco.'

'Little Sir Eco, how do you do,' said Cynthia. 'I think we've basically got it. Can you write eight in two months?'

'Eight what?' asked Henry.

'Eight fifty-two-minute episodes,' said Joss Pride.

'I don't actually start teaching again until the end of September,' said Henry. 'But I did actually promise to write a piece for an adult education journal on the style of late Pinter.'

'Late Pinter, he's great,' said Cynthia.

'But I could put it aside,' said Henry.

'You could put it in,' said Cynthia.

'Yes, I do believe I could ... schedule it,' said Henry.

'Fine,' said Jocelyn Pride. 'So if I call back your agent?'

'My agent?' said Henry, who had almost forgotten he had one.

'Kenneth Stoke-Patrick,' said Jocelyn. 'She's the one who suggested your name.'

Henry remembered her now, a very bright and go-ahead lady who had approached him and said she could further his career, and whom he had met once or twice for a drink in the bar of the Groucho Club, while she was waiting to take some famous American novelist and his or her usual bronzed lover into lunch. 'Ah, did she?' he said.

'We told her we were looking for an unknown writer of genius who wasn't already fully booked out for the summer, and she came straight out with your name,' said Cynthia, taking out her credit card and handing it to the waiter. 'Hey, come on, you'd better come and meet Lord Mellow. He's flying off to London shortly for the BAFTA awards. He doesn't like people to be late.'

On the fortieth floor of the great glass tower, Lord

Mellow stood in his underpants again in the office in the penthouse suite, as secretaries brought him clothes for his next social duty.

'My dear fellow,' said Lord Mellow, taking Henry by the arm and leading him into the room, 'so now you have come into my employ!'

'Subject to contract, yes,' said Henry, remembering that his agent had told him once, in the Groucho, just before John Updike came in, to start all sentences like this.

'Take that as read,' said Lord Mellow. 'What I want I get. Now I hope these talented young people explained the nature of this crucial venture fully. What we are looking for is a major prize-winning project that will transform the entire history of the television drama serial. I want art, I want feeling. I want worldwide sales and likeable people. I want it shot in a lush foreign location where you can get malt whisky.'

'Oh, I see,' said Cynthia. 'You're going to produce?'

'Yes,' said Lord Mellow. 'I intend to be Executive Producer on this myself, the kind that doesn't do much but gets a separate screen credit. Quite, Cynthia?'

'Quite,' said the Head of Productions.

'I want stars so famous nobody could believe we can afford them and a central character who doesn't speak at all. Jeremy Irons said nothing in *Brideshead* and it made him famous. I know a trend when I see one.'

'Quite,' said Cynthia.

'I want a director who shoots the scenes very slowly with lots of high crane shots, and that means definitely not Mark Hasper,' said Lord Mellow. 'And how many are we talking?'

'Eight,' said Jocelyn Pride.

'No, we're not, we're talking ten,' said Lord Mellow. 'Anyone who doesn't think big isn't big enough for Eldorado.'

'But we're shooting in the autumn,' said Jocelyn Pride.

'So we start shooting without all the scripts in,' said Lord Mellow. 'That's a trend too.'

'You want me to write *ten* scripts now?' said Henry, finding the drink was wearing off. 'But my university term starts again in September. I don't think I could possibly ...'

'Ah, you're a don of some kind,' said Lord Mellow.

'I'm a lecturer,' said Henry.

'Fascinating,' said Lord Mellow. 'I considered becoming Master of a Cambridge college myself. Until I realised no man in his right mind could possibly afford it. Come with me.'

Lord Mellow took Henry's elbow again and propelled him toward the window, which reached down to floor level and had an unpleasant quality of seeming not to be there at all.

'Now, take a look down there and tell me what you see,' said Lord Mellow.

What Henry saw was a vertiginous drop, for the Eldorado tower dwarfed the great city, rising not only above the roofs but above the birds themselves, which flew about desperately below. Far below the birds moved the people, the traffic, and the city: dwarf red buses, Dinky cars, small toy people moved through an elaborate maze of existence.

'All of human life,' suggested Henry, feeling that was the right sort of thing to say.

'Ah, that,' said Lord Mellow. 'But do you know what those buildings are?'

He pointed to some small and decaying Victorian premises with pinnacles and domes that stood dully in the great shadow cast by the high glass tower. Guano caked the lead roofs, grass grew lushly in the gutterings, broken roof-lights stared up at them.

'That is the local university,' said Lord Mellow. 'I particularly wanted the site next to that. It reminds me, you see, each time I look down, that we at Eldorado also have our educational functions and responsibilities. In fact we draw on the services of those chaps down there to put on an afternoon educational programme each weekday. Perhaps you've seen it.'

'Actually I don't have ...' said Henry.

'There must be one going out at this minute,' said Lord Mellow.

Lord Mellow turned on a television set, and a small moustached figure prated on for a moment about Jane Austen, until Lord Mellow grew suddenly impatient and turned it off again.

'It also reminds me we have a hell of a lot more money,' he said. 'Young man, forget your futile teaching. Take a leave, have a sabbatical, throw in the towel, claim your pension, ask for a golden handshake. We'll need you right through the shoot, for rewrites and re-re-rewrites. What ridiculous sum do they pay you?'

Henry murmured the nature of his salary, and Lord Mellow laughed.

'Good God,' he said, 'two scripts will earn you that. One, if we sell this to America, Australia, everywhere in the world. And we will. We're not talking piddle here. Call your agent. He'll tell you this is one of those offers you can't refuse. Every writer in the country would give his nose for it. The greatest drama series in the entire history of television!'

Just then a helicopter flew close by the window and could be heard making a terrifying noise as it landed on the adjacent roof. Wind blew papers off Lord Mellow's desk; a secretary quickly held out some trousers in front of him and he stepped into them. Another held out his dinner jacket; another stood in front of him and tied his bow-tie.

'Right, I must cut and run,' said Lord Mellow, opening a drawer in his desk which was filled with money, and loading his pockets with it. 'I'm off to the BAFTA awards. Nothing, alas, for us this year ...'

'As usual,' murmured Cynthia Hyde-Lemon.

'But next year I want to be up there on stage, running away with every award in the business for this prestigious project,' said Lord Mellow, pulling on a hairnet. 'So I greatly look forward to working with you in a mutual way, Mr Whoever you are. All I want is for this to be the biggest show ever.'

'And I want it cheap,' murmured Cynthia Hyde-Lemon.

'Oh, and I want it cheap,' said Lord Mellow, as he donned a helmet, straightened his bow-tie, and ran out to the helicopter.

6

At the small provincial university where Henry Babbacombe performed the duties of Lecturer in English and Drama in the Department of Extra-Mural Studies, they were cutting almost everything.

They were cutting the numbers of students, cutting the courses, cutting the secretaries, cutting the porters; they were cutting the playing fields, cutting the student accommodation, cutting the library, cutting the teaching buildings. They were also cutting the staff. There were those who suspected that the people in the university administration – who, as it happened, were not on the whole being cut – were undertaking the exercise with almost an excess of enthusiasm, as if they had been longing for the day when the troublesome professoriate, the finicky lecturers, the annoying readers, would pass on to pastures new, mostly in the United States.

Perhaps it was unfortunate that the Vice-Chancellor, who was, like many Vice-Chancellors, a disappointed scientist, had been newly knighted by the current Prime Minister, and therefore felt himself peculiarly privy to the inmost workings of her mind. Certainly he was himself an enthusiastic privatiser, or privateer, and that summer of 1986 'privatisation' was, along with 'buzz-word', the great buzz-word. For a year or more he had been thriving on all sorts of novel ideas of this kind, encouraging, for example, sponsored tutorials, so that lecturers now discussed the poems of Catullus or mathematical equations wearing teeshirts and little caps that said on them 'Boots' or 'Babycham'. In all the corridors now, there were big notices saying, 'The faculty in this university all wear Marks and Spencers underwear.' More boldly, he had been trying to get all the chairs in the university endowed, by commercial organisations, or even private individuals: the Westland Chair of Anglo-American Relations, the Kingsley Amis Chair of Women's Studies, and the Durex Chair of French Letters were only some of the ideas he was presently developing. Stirred by pressure from the government to bring in more relevant subjects, he was trying to disestablish ancient departments like Classics and English altogether, and replace them by more modern ones, such as a Department of Snooker Studies.

These were only some of the ideas by which he hoped to transform a loss-making traditional institution into one more fitted to the world of today. Since overseas students do not count as conventional students, and bring in extra income, he had been striving, with enormous enthusiasm and enterprise, to get them. Members of faculty now spent most of their lives sitting in hotels and motels in Hong Kong and the United States with videotapes of a sunlit pastoral campus, making premium offers on junior year abroad courses which included tours of the Tower of London, hideaway weekends in Paris, and courses on Shakespeare and the English Folk-Dance that few of the faculty were physically equipped to teach. More cleverly still, he had somehow persuaded the immigration service to slip gaily-illustrated leaflets into the passports of non-nationals as they arrived at the British air and sea ports, advertising the university's ambitious offerings. The

entire countryside neighbouring the university was now
filled with wandering bands of Malays and Vietnamese,
halting the locals and asking them in strange accents
where to find the university, which few had heard of
anyway. Alas, by the time they found it at last they were
frequently disappointed; for the attractive courses had
already been – well, cut.

As Henry Babbacombe parked his Morris Traveller in
the summer-empty university car-park, he could see
men removing from the great building in front of him the
sign that said 'Library', and replacing it with another
that said 'Center for Overseas Students'. It was the day
following his exciting visit to Eldorado, and a certain
gloom was setting in. The Leoville-Barton had worn off,
there was in his throat a strange taste rather like a rancid
kiwi fruit, and he had had yet another sleepless night,
this time filled not only with the roar of combine
harvesters but with strange and terrible thoughts. There
was the thought that, foregoing his normal academic
discretion, he had somehow been tempted into corrupt-
ing his integrity with the dross of commerce. There was
the thought that, for reasons he could no longer clearly
recall, he had committed himself to writing, soon and at
the greatest speed, a major series for television, running
for ten hours or so, on a dramatic topic which he could
not remember, and about which he had no serious ideas
whatsoever, except for the fact that its general colour
was supposed to be puce. There was the thought, or
rather the dark realisation, that this meant working
under the executive control of Lord Mellow, a man who
even Henry could see was of somewhat volatile moods.
And there was the further thought, or rather the certain
knowledge, that the only way to do all this was to act as

Lord Mellow had suggested, and ask his head of department, the Professor of Adult Education, for a term's leave of absence without advance warning, so throwing the autumn academic programme into considerable chaos.

But Professor Finniston was a kindly and understanding man, much concerned for the future of his staff. When Henry had first joined his department he had taken him aside, in the most kindly and thoughtful of ways, and explained to him that to be a university teacher was a great privilege, and that this accounted for the fact that the salary was designed only to support a single man in celibate circumstances. 'That has always been the academic tradition,' he said. 'When I started, university teachers all had private incomes. And none of us married. We understood then that genitals are a great distraction to scholarship.' From that time forward he had always been a wise master and friend, and Henry Babbacombe sometimes thought that it was precisely because he had followed Professor Finniston's wise advice that he had actually become a writer, there being, of course, little else to do with himself.

Even so, it was with some trepidation that Babbacombe now made his way to the Extra-Mural Department – which, with great appropriateness, was off the campus altogether, and flourished, or otherwise, in an old Victorian house which lay a good way down the main road. It looked peculiarly empty as Henry went in, but then it always did in the late summer, when even the odd summer school was over, and the winter programme had not begun. In this halcyon space academic writers write their books, usually finding it necessary first to do some research on the châteaux of the Dordogne or the retsinas of Greece. Dust therefore hung in the air, most offices were empty, and in the hall great book-boxes, designed for winter courses in outlying districts, the hard work to come in the term still some way off, lay waiting to be filled.

But Professor Finniston was there, as he always was. His office door was wide open, and the patter of one-finger typing sounded from within.

Babbacombe tapped on the open door.

'Come,' said Professor Finniston, looking up. 'Ah, Babbacombe.'

Professor Finniston was a fat man, but like everyone and everything else he seemed to have grown thinner over the summer. He looked over his typewriter and beamed, and Babbacombe knew that no one would have a better understanding of his problems, or be better able to advise him.

'Professor Finniston, could I have a word?' said Babbacombe. 'I'd just like to ask your advice, as a friend.'

'Of course, young man. Move those cup-cakes off the chair and sit yourself down,' said Professor Finniston, taking off his spectacles. 'And how may I be of help?'

'I'm in something of a difficulty,' said Henry. 'And rather uncertain what to do.'

'My word, are you, Babbacombe?' said Finniston kindly. 'And what is the young lady's name? More to the point, is she litigious? I fear most of them are nowadays.'

'It's not that, actually, Professor Finniston.'

'If not that, then what?' asked Finniston. 'Most of the problems I encounter are either those of fornication or else of plagiarism. Now it is said we have a royal case of the latter. Alas that no one had whispered in that noble ear the simple word 'intertextuality'. Very well, if it is the latter ...'

'It isn't that either,' said Babbacombe. 'Professor Finniston, I have been approached by a television company. Do you know what that is?'

'I have a vague idea,' said Finniston. 'Do go on.'

'They wish me to write a series for them, of the dramatic kind.'

'My word, do they, my boy?' said Finniston. 'And what on earth alerted them to your decidedly bushel-hidden light?'

'My – well, agent,' said Babbacombe.

'Oh, you have one of those, do you?' said Finniston, looking at him with a new respect. 'I have written twenty-five books and always managed without one. Of course I have never made a penny piece, indeed in most cases a considerable loss. But then, unlike our present Vice-Chancellor, I would never dream of hiring out my mind for vulgar profit.'

'It's a very tempting offer,' said Babbacombe. 'But what it does mean is that I should have to ask you for leave of absence next term.'

Professor Finniston stared at him.

'Really?' he said slowly. 'You mean, you would simply leave me stranded, without a lecturer, and with five difficult classes a week in remote districts to cover as best I might?'

'Well, yes, I'm afraid ...' said Babbacombe.

'I see,' said Finniston. 'Well, well, this *is* good news.'

'It is?' said Babbacombe.

'Oh yes,' said Finniston, rising from his chair. 'You see, Babbacombe, while you have been strumming away at your word-processor all summer, setting down your strange and solitary fantasies, we here have been going through misery. Our eminent University Grants Committee chose to write a report on all the universities. As perhaps you know already, if the daily press ever reaches you wherever it is you live.'

'I had heard,' said Henry. 'I gather they rather want to cut ...'

'They want to butcher, to lay waste, to destroy,' said Finniston. 'You probably also saw they chose to give ratings to the various departments and universities in the country. Rather as if they were running some Michelin Guide to thought. They gave the best departments stars, and so on. They did have the decency to describe the enterprise as 'approximate', though the technical word for it is 'cock-up'. Alas, Babbacombe, I fear we here did not do well out of it.'

'No?' said Babbacombe.

'No,' said Professor Finniston. 'All our departments got daggers. It was hardly a surprise. We are very northern, and remote from the railway line. To my knowledge none of the sub-committees the UGC sent out to examine us has ever succeeded in reaching us. Our reputation is, like most, all gossip, and I fear gossip has never favoured us.'

'Why is that?' asked Babbacombe.

'My dear fellow,' said Finniston, 'we have never deigned to *boast* of our reputation, like the vulgar new universities. And you know many of my colleagues have always refused to publish books, naturally preferring to transfer their thoughts by word of mouth to the two or three people who are fit to understand them.'

'Quite,' said Babbacombe.

'Alas, it all bodes quite ill, Babbacombe, very ill,' said Finniston. 'The Vice-Chancellor is in Mauritius now, trying to come to terms with it. It has already meant many losses.'

'Oh, dear,' said Henry Babbacombe.

'Professor Porritt in French – you recall him, the Methodist Structuralist? He made all his staff sign the pledge, and called his daughters Langue and Parole?'

'Yes, I do,' said Babbacombe.

'Well, he was put in charge of golden handshakes. So he gave himself one, and now I hear he's opening a French restaurant in Dufford. To be called for some reason the Mise-En-Abîme. As for Professor Harris of English – you know, the hairy Shakespearean?'

Babbacombe nodded.

'He has taken early retirement, and is retraining as an airline pilot. Professor Festinger of Physics has run off with a ballet dancer, we are not sure of which sex. And my budget has been cut by twenty per cent.'

'That's terrible,' said Babbacombe.

'So this televisual enterprise,' said Professor Finniston, 'I take it they will reimburse you quite well for it? I understand these ventures are quite costly.'

'I believe the budget for the programme is about eight million pounds,' said Babbacombe modestly.

Professor Finniston looked at him in amazement, and wiped his brow with a handkerchief.

'Good God, man,' he said. 'Good God. You realise you could start a university of your own for that?'

'Yes, but that's not what it's for,' said Babbacombe.

'Oh, no, that's never what it's for,' said Finniston. 'What *is* it for?'

'I'm not quite sure,' said Babbacombe. 'Art. Puce-coloured art with a strong story line.'

Professor Finniston sat down again.

'And doubtless of this superfluity you will yourself take

a fair cut?'

'Of course, I have to discuss it with my –'

'This agent person who looks after the base affairs of your life,' said Finniston. 'Quite. Clearly we live in two different worlds, Babbacombe. Though I suppose these days most people do.'

'Well, I imagine, in the circumstances, if I was to take a term off that would relieve things a bit,' said Henry Babbacombe. 'It could be quite fortunate all round, really.'

'Babbacombe,' said Finniston, 'it is my sad duty to have to cut out two members of staff. I have been desperately hoping all summer that two of my colleagues would be hit by buses on the street. I've kept sending them out every day on dangerous errands, but I fear my weak little stratagem has not worked at all. Well, I do believe the bus has come at last. Clearly in the circumstances you have no more need of us.'

Babbacombe stared at him.

'But I do,' he said. 'I'm not the sort of person to let fame go to my head. I'm not a commercial person, integrity is my watchword. I'm really a teacher, I write on the side ...'

'We all have to turn sides to middle, these days,' said Professor Finniston. 'How fortunate, that your triumph should coincide so exactly with our desire to be rid of you.'

'Of me? But why should I be the one ...?' asked Babbacombe. 'You've always said I'm one of the best people in the department.'

'Quite,' said Finniston. 'Why indeed? If academic merit were the matter, there could be no question. Certainly you are one of our best and most alert members of staff.

That is why I have been recommending you for promotion up to now.'

'So why not one of the others?' asked Babbacombe.

'Exactly. Why not Dr Mucklethwaite, who has never had a mind to speak of and is totally incompetent? But he has seven small children, all of them cripples, he assures me. Or why not Miss Battle, endlessly incapacitated by her endless nervous breakdowns and her agoraphobia? But who in all decency could upset her further? And being a woman, however hopeless, she is all too likely to sue. No, Babbacombe, you are the one able-bodied member of the department. I fear we must turn to you. After all, you have no dependents. All you do is write in a shed all day.'

'You were the one who advised me not to marry,' said Babbacombe. 'You said a university teacher couldn't afford to.'

'Quite,' said Finniston. 'And you see now how far-sighted I was.'

Finniston rose and held out his hand.

'I only wish this handshake could be golden,' he said warmly. 'However, you have no need of that. You are a great model of Thatcherite enterprise, and I congratulate you. I shall look forward to reading of your Queen's Award for Industry in the non-academic columns of *The Times* one of these days.'

'But I haven't decided to accept the television contract,' said Babbacombe. 'I just wanted to talk it over informally with you. And anyway I do have tenure ...'

'I do hope you're not thinking of suing us,' said Professor Finniston. 'You did just attempt to break your contract. And in this uncertain world there is one certain thing. This university has no money, none at all. No, good luck, young man. I am certain you are doing the right thing. After all, hasn't my advice always been sound?'

So Babbacombe went out of the door; and Professor Finniston rubbed his hands, and sat down to his one-finger typing again.

7

In the recently cut prairie fields that lay just over the hedge from Henry Babbacombe's garden shed, they were, quite evidently, spreading muck.

The leaves were beginning to turn, the nights closing in; in Henry's old shed the field mice who had taken charge of the wastepaper basket were bedding down for a chill winter. The harvest-mites had gone, but the smell of agricultural dung penetrated with an even greater intensity. On the rough wooden wall above his desk, Henry Babbacombe had pinned a set of little notes about the duties of the summer. There were reminders about the article on the very late Pinter, as well as a couple of book reviews that he had promised to *Al Fresco: The Journal of Extra-Mural Studies* for the end of the vacation. There were sheets with various abstract ciphers and hieroglyphs, the working notes for his yellow-coloured novel.

Now it seemed unlikely that any of these tasks would ever be done. For evidently writing for television bore no relation whatsoever to the quiet, contemplative activity Henry had always thought writing was, and up to now had always found it, belonging in some quite different realm of creative adventure altogether. When writers are writing a novel, or crafting a scholarly article, as Henry had throughout his literary existence, they generally like silence and solitude, a quiet space in a quiet place; that was why he had taken to his garden shed. But television writing was apparently done amidst an end-

less hubbub of noise, activity, interference and recrimi-
nation which in his case started in the Eldorado tower
but spilled freely over into the shed itself. From the
instant that Henry had begun to attempt work on the
project there had simply not been what Mrs Raper liked
to call a moment's peace.

First there had been the long crisis about the contract,
which had kept Henry's agent, the girl called Kenneth,
on the telephone for hours every day, discussing problems about residuals in Puerto Rico he did not even begin
to understand. When a man on an express motor-bicycle
eventually appeared in the garden, with a copy of an
extended legal document that Henry gathered he was
supposed to sign, and Henry went into the house to
telephone Kenneth, there were more baffling mysteries.
The series had, for example, somehow acquired a title,
Serious Damage, that had certainly not come from him;
Kenneth said that this was simply a working title,
necessary for the purpose of writing a contract. The fee
quoted was a good deal less than the sum that had been
talked about at the firehouse lunch and in Lord Mellow's
office; Kenneth explained that this was because she had
reserved many rights for the author which would prove
benison beyond belief when the series was shown, and
that in any case no one had ever heard of him. The
delivery date for the scripts was shown as the end of
September, but Kenneth explained that this was simply
notional. Henry was to have no say over choice of
director, casting or the final form of the script; Kenneth
said that this was perfectly usual, especially since Henry
did not know any directors or actors anyway. Henry was
required to do as many rewrites as was required until the
script was finally approved; Kenneth said that that was

the way television worked, or at least that was her impression, since she had never actually had to do a television contract before. The document also described the series as being in 13×1 episodes; Kenneth said that was just a point still up for discussion. The man on the motor-cycle said that he hoped to return to England before it got dark, at which Henry sighed and, getting out his pen, signed.

After that, the telephone had never stopped ringing, for evidently it was a well-known law of series that, the moment an author sits at his desk to write, that very movement will set the telephones working. The instant Henry placed himself before the keyboard of the Remington Portable and raised his fingers aloft, Mrs Raper would come banging on the shed door. Henry would run up the overgrown path, past the decaying roses, through the ripe smell of dung, and gasp into the mouthpiece. His work, of course, had been interrupted by telephones before – by messages saying that the shoes left for repair six months previously were now ready for collection, or changing an appointment for a haircut. But these calls were different. They came not just from desks and callboxes but from cars, and trains, and planes. They came in the middle of the night; they came, it could be guaranteed, the moment he ever went near the lavatory.

They emanated from strange parties with unusual requests. A girl who said she was costumes called every morning around seven and discussed wigs for the characters, even though Henry had not invented any characters yet and was not sure if he wanted to make it a story with people in it. A young man who said he was a location finder kept calling from Venice, describing various splendid palazzi which he said would be ideal for the third episode. A terribly insistent man called Webber kept calling to talk for hours every day about the musical concepts he was putting in the series, even though Henry said he was not intending to include any music in the series and was wondering whether to make the whole thing silent. A man called Roger Trothammer, who said he was the Prod. Ass., kept ringing about budgets and costings, asking peculiar questions about how long they would have to be in India and what types of aircraft would be needed for the flying sequences; sometimes he just called and made irritable remarks. A lot of actors rang and said they had read about the project in *Broadcast* and would he write parts for them in it, and several people from the village came by and said they had Equity cards and wanted to be extras. A television team from another company rang and asked if they could film him writing the script. A zoo rang and offered him lions. Jocelyn Pride came on constantly, asking for an outline of a synopsis or else a plan of a treatment.

But above all there was Lord Mellow, who seemed to ring hourly from car and helicopter phones in strange places, and in a mercurial variety of moods. Sometimes he was elated and extravagant, saying that what Henry was writing was probably the greatest thing he had ever read, even though he had not yet seen it, despite the passage of two weeks. Sometimes he was generous and forgiving, realising that Henry was probably even now fine-tuning the thirteen episodes and he had better allow him another couple of days before delivery. Sometimes he was enraged, violently shouting questions down the line that Henry found impossible to answer, such as whether he had gone totally out of his head and flushed ten million pounds down the toilet.

The telephone rang so often that Henry had scarcely had time to give the script itself a thought, though he had had some important dreams about it, and now realised that it would not be so much puce as a colour more resembling maroon. Today, though, three weeks after his first visit to Eldorado Television, things had seemed rather quieter. So Henry got into the car and drove the twenty miles to the nearby small town where he got his toilet paper and his Valpolicella, and there in the small bookstore he purchased a small book called *Film and Television Writing for Beginners* which Kenneth had told him she was finding very interesting. It sat beside his typewriter now, filled with depressing advice about how to make a plan, draw up an outline, make a synopsis, present a treatment and handle rewrites. But all this seemed too late now; the important thing was to get the script done. Henry put the book on the top of the typewriter, read a very long chapter about the importance of keeping scenes very short, and then found what he was looking for. At the back was a page about format and technique, all about cuts and intercuts and match cuts and cut tos and cutaways and voice overs and tracking shots. Henry pressed the page open, put it beside the Remington Portable, and started to type:

SERIOUS DAMAGE
By Henry Babbacombe

EPISODE ONE
Act One

he wrote. Then he looked at the format instructions, and wrote again:

63

1/1. INT. PHOTO-BOOTH. DAY.

A., A MAN SMALL RATHER THAN TALL, SOMEWHERE
BETWEEN THIRTY AND SIXTY, SITS IN THE BOOTH
LOOKING AT THE PASSPORT PHOTO CAMERA. HE IS
CLEARLY WORRIED ABOUT THE FUTURE. HE HAS A
TRAVEL-BAG OVER HIS SHOULDER. THE SOUND OF
TRAINS AND WHISTLES INDICATES THAT THIS IS A
RAILWAY STATION. A VOICE CALLS IN AN
UNKNOWN FOREIGN LANGUAGE FROM OUTSIDE THE
BOOTH. THE MAN TURNS. THE CAMERA FLASHES.
CUT TO:

1/2. EXT. FOREIGN RAILWAY STATION. DAY.

A LARGE INTERNATIONAL RAILWAY STATION WITH
MANY TRAINS AND BUSTLING PASSENGERS. ARMED
GUARDS WALK AMONG THE PASSENGERS AND SOME
ARE POSTED ON THE GANTRIES OVER THE STATION
CONCOURSES.
AN ATMOSPHERE OF SINISTER UNEASE.
THE CAMERA PANS TOWARD A PHOTO-BOOTH.
INSIDE THE LIGHT FLASHES.
CUT TO:
B., A MAN IN A BIG HAT WATCHES THE BOOTH
FROM BEHIND A NEWSPAPER.
CUT TO:
C., A YOUNG AND ATTRACTIVE WOMAN IN BLACK
WATCHES THE BOOTH FROM ANOTHER POSITION.
CUT TO:
D., ANOTHER MAN IN A BIG HAT WATCHES THE
WOMAN.

AN ATMOSPHERE OF INDESCRIBABLE MENACE, IF
NOT ANTICIPATION.
CUT TO:

1/3. EXT. PHOTO-BOOTH, RAILWAY STATION. DAY.

THE PHOTOGRAPHS SLIDE OUT INTO THE TRAY.
CLOSE SHOT:
THE PHOTOGRAPHS: THEY ARE BLANK!
CUT TO:
THE WOMAN, C., HURRYING FORWARD. SHE
SNATCHES THE PHOTOGRAPHS FROM THE TRAY.
SHE HURRIES OFF WITH THEM THROUGH THE DENSE
CROWDS.
CUT TO:
D. FOLLOWING HER.
CUT TO:
A. COMES OUT OF THE BOOTH, LOOKS FOR THE
PHOTOGRAPHS.
AN ATMOSPHERE OF BAFFLEMENT.
THEN A. GLIMPSES THE WOMAN DISAPPEARING
THROUGH THE CROWDS. HE HURRIES OFF AFTER
HER.
CUT TO:
B. FOLDING UP HIS PAPER AND FOLLOWING A.
AN ATMOSPHERE OF IMPENDING DOOM.
CUT TO:

1/4. INT. STUDY, A.'S HOUSE. DAY.

AN OLD ENGLISH HOUSE IN AN OLD ENGLISH

GARDEN. BIRDS TWITTER HAPPILY.

AN ATMOSPHERE OF COMFORTABLE ELEGANCE.

THE MAN, A., LOOKING YOUNGER, SITS IN AN ELEGANT STUDY BEHIND A FINE OLD DESK. HE TYPES ON A VERY NEW REMINGTON PORTABLE.

CLOSE SHOT:

THE WORDS HE IS TYPING. THEY ARE IN AN UNKNOWN FOREIGN LANGUAGE!

A. APPARENTLY LOSES INSPIRATION. HE STOPS TYPING AND THINKS. HIS MIND CHURNS. HE SEEMS TO BE REMEMBERING SOMETHING, PERHAPS FROM HIS CHILDHOOD. BUT THE WORDS WILL NOT COME. HE GRASPS AT ONE THOUGHT, THEN ANOTHER. IN DESPERATION HE RISES TO HIS FEET AND GOES TO THE WINDOW.

AN ATMOSPHERE OF INTELLECTUAL CONFUSION.

FROM HIS POINT-OF-VIEW (POV) WE SEE A VERY BEAUTIFUL GIRL, E., IN A SKIMPY BATHING SUIT LYING ON A SUN LOUNGER IN THE ELEGANT GARDEN. SHE IS DRINKING AN ICED DRINK AND READING A BOOK. SHE TURNS OVER ONTO HER STOMACH, LYING FACING TOWARD THE HOUSE.

CUTAWAY SHOT:

A. FROM THE POV OF E.

AN ATMOSPHERE OF EROTIC EXPECTATION.

CUT TO:

1/5. EXT. GARDEN, A.'S HOUSE. DAY.

THE GIRL, E., READING HER BOOK, AND LOOKING UP TO GLANCE AT THE HOUSE. SHE PUTS DOWN THE BOOK. WE SEE THE TITLE IS IN YET ANOTHER UNKNOWN FOREIGN LANGUAGE!

AN ATMOSPHERE OF MYSTERY.
IN THE HOUSE WE CAN SEE A. IN HIS STUDY, PACING
DESPERATELY.
A. FROM THE POV OF E.
CUT TO:

1/6. INT. UPSTAIRS STUDY, A.'S HOUSE. DAY.

E. FROM THE POV OF A.
A. STARES DOWN AT THE MYSTERIOUS WRITING.
AN ATMOSPHERE OF ANXIETY.
SUDDENLY THE TELEPH –

'Telephone,' said Mrs Raper, barging into the garden
shed. 'There isn't a moment's peace. And I can't be
running up and down this path twenty times a day at my
age, Mr Babbacombe, and that's flat. You ought to get
yourself one of those phoneless cords, they make them,
you know.'

'Who is it this time?' asked Henry, rising from the
milking stool.

'That Lord Mellow from the Eldorado again,' said Mrs
Raper.

'I'll come,' said Henry.

'Too late, he rang off,' said Mrs Raper. 'He was calling
from Prince Rainier's of Monaco and he didn't want to
run up a large bill.'

'What did he want?' asked Henry.

'He wanted you over at the Eldorado office first thing
tomorrow morning for a production meeting to discuss
the whole project.'

'How can I go over there tomorrow?' said Henry. 'I'm
supposed to be working on the script. It's not easy

writing for television, you know.'

'I *don't* know, Mr Babbacombe,' said Mrs Raper. 'I can't even write myself a proper letter. He just said if you wasn't there first thing he'd hire a new writer.'

'But it takes a five-hour journey on the train to get there!' said Henry. 'The only way I could do it is to drive all night.'

'What you need is one of these helicopeters,' said Mrs Raper. 'They make them, you know.'

'I know,' said Henry. 'Lord Mellow's got one.'

'Ask him to come to you, then,' said Mrs Raper.

Henry looked round the garden shed. The field-mice were very noisy in the wastepaper basket. A vile wind was blowing through the knot-holes in the walls. The smell of dung was growing ever stronger.

'No,' he said. 'I'd better go to him.'

'Well, I've got to go and cut Jack's tea,' said Mrs Raper. 'What with answering your phone, I've got nothing shifted these last three weeks. And you used to be such a nice quiet person to do for. Now I just don't know what to expect next.'

'I don't know myself,' said Henry, snatching the pages from the typewriter and putting them in his briefcase. 'Writing for television isn't what I expected. I sometimes think I'm not cut out for it at all.'

''Course you are, Mr Babbacombe,' said Mrs Raper, with steadfast village loyalty. 'The rubbish they put on the televisions nowadays, any idiot could do it, even you, Mr Babbacombe.'

'That's very kind of you, Mrs Raper,' said Henry, looking at her gratefully. And, his briefcase packed, he went out to pump up the tyres of the tired Morris Traveller, and make it all ready for his long drive through the moorland night.

8

When Henry Babbacombe made his second arrival at the
great glass tower that housed Eldorado Television, he did
not, it has to be admitted, cut nearly as much of a dash as
before.

The long and troubling journey across the bumpy,
mountainous spinal cord of England proved no simpler
by car than by train, and no more pleasant by night than
by day. Great howling winds troubled the moorland tops,
a baleful moon shone red, and just before dawn Henry's
Traveller bumped into a very large sheep that had
chosen to pass the night in the middle of the road. The
animal, after Henry had extricated it, appeared unhurt,
though angry, and ran off into the darkness, bleating
blasphemously. The car had done worse, and Henry's
radiator promptly leaked out its contents. By the time the
meeting at Eldorado began, Henry was still completing a
three-hour wait for a small village garage to open, and it
was another two hours before the repair was complete.
Henry decided to cut across to the motorway, beset by
flood, tempest and a plague of savage lorries. These
passed him at lunatic speeds in the fast lane, flashing
great lights, spraying him with sheets of water, every
kind of detritus, and finally a hail of gravel which
shattered his windscreen. That took another hour to
mend, and it was already early afternoon by the time
that Henry reached the great steaming city that was his
destination. Here he spent another futile hour, circu-
lating a devious and obscure one-way system that

spiralled round the Eldorado building. The great glass
tower rose above him, ever visible, never attainable.
Finally Henry disposed of his car in a concrete, graffiti-
daubed multi-storey carpark, and, his briefcase on his
head, made the last stage of his journey on foot through
the pouring rain.

There was a short-cut through the courts and
archways of the great Victorian university, and Henry
took it. The great Gothic buildings, much blackened by
the industrial smoke that had largely financed them in
the first place, stood silent, for evidently in the world of
academic life the peace of vacation, the ideal time in the
university calendar, continued. Something like a hal-
lowed silence reigned. A few dirty pigeons cooed malevo-
lently at him from the sagging gutterings, and from the
stone head of the statue of the founding Victorian
philanthropist that rose up like a ghost in the middle of
the court. The bell in the broken clock tower bronchiti-
cally croaked out the turning hour. Someone without
musical ability was practising the bassoon. A few notices
flapped away on a board, announcing essay com-
petitions on whether there should be a third sex or
pointing directions to a place where one could give one's
blood. The campus was quite different from Henry's own,
and yet he felt at once at home in the distinctive world of
intellectual contemplation, quietude, mannered eccen-
tricity, and indifference to sad and foolish reality, which
quite simply, he felt, represented the best of all human
life. It was the world in which he truly knew he belonged,
and the world from which, because of the cuts, he had
now been excluded. Sad at heart, he walked on through
the rain toward the moneyed modern world of glass and
concrete. The self-operating glass doors of Eldorado

operated before he had even reached them, and let him in.

It was already that time of a late afternoon when busy television executives leaving the building after a hard day's work cross over in the foyer with yet more busy television executives stumbling back after a hard day's working lunch. Henry let himself be tested by security and went to the desk. The Chinese girl there wrote out his security pass and directed him to Jocelyn Pride's office without even looking up at him, as if she knew already that his reputation was in decline. There was no one in the least amusing in the glass lift. Cast adrift in the waiting room outside Pride's office, he had to wait for half an hour in a long row of bedraggled writers with worn scripts on their knees, a group of haggard actors waiting to read parts they knew they would never get, and a man who after ten minutes proved to have come to mend the photocopier. No one said anything to Henry, or offered him coffee, decaffeinated or otherwise. And when Pride, more tousle-headed and brown-suited than ever, opened his office door and summoned Henry inside, his manner seemed indifferent, if not actually brusque.

'You're fucking late, Henry,' he said. 'Lord Mellow doesn't like being kept waiting.'

'He's not still waiting, is he?' asked Henry. 'I'm sorry I'm so late. I bumped into a sheep on the moors.'

'We can smell it, Henry,' said Pride. 'Lord Mellow had to cut and run. He flew out at lunchtime for a meeting of gnomes, in Zurich. But before he went he did leave a message for you, if you ever turned up.'

'Ah,' said Henry. 'What's that?'

'Tell that bastard to get his ass off the chair and give me those scripts,' recited Jocelyn Pride.

'But the scripts aren't due in until the end of September,' said Henry. 'And even that's cutting it a bit fine.'

'We scrapped that schedule at the production meeting this morning,' said Jocelyn Pride. 'Frankly that's impossible, if we're going to shoot in the autumn and transmit in the spring.'

'But I can't do them any sooner,' said Henry. 'A writer has to let his inspiration take its course.'

'I hope you're not trying to say Lord Mellow doesn't respect the writer,' said Jocelyn Pride. 'Lord Mellow is world-famous for respecting the writer. He's respected Pinter and Stoppard and Beckett. He's respected Shakespeare and Molière and Euripides. He's respected them; and they've respected him. But he does expect them to be totally professional, and get their inspiration in on time, if not before. This is very distressing, Henry. Don't you have anything for us, anything?'

'I've brought a bit of it along,' said Henry, reaching into his briefcase and taking out the few pages he had stuffed there. 'Just so we could discuss the initial concept . . .'

'I knew you were great underneath, Henry!' cried Jocelyn Pride, slapping him on the arm and shouting loudly to his secretary to come in. 'Babs, make a hundred copies of that and distribute them round the team.'

'Of course it's all very tentative and really only a few preliminary suggestions, to get the feel,' said Henry. 'What team is that?'

'The team that's planning *Serious Damage*,' said Jocelyn Pride. 'Come with me and I'll show you.'

Pride seized Henry by the arm and hurried him out through a back door into a long corridor. At the end of the corridor were some large double doors, and on the doors was a large notice, which said *Serious Damage: Production Office*. Pride pushed Henry through the doors, and inside he saw a great room, filled with activity. About fifty desks were in it, some with moveable screens round them, some with telexes or word-processors on them, some stacked with television monitors. People sat at the desks, creative-looking people in creative-looking clothes. Some of them typed. Some of them were making small models of rooms. Some of them read books. Some of them drew maps. Some of them held up photographs. Most of them were drinking tea or coffee from plastic cups. Nearly all of them were on the telephone.

'That's the team,' said Pride proudly. 'Those over there are design, those are costume and props, those are production co-ordination, those are transport, those are casting, those are locations, those are finance. They're brilliant people, brilliant. Lord Mellow has hired them for enormous sums. They could be in Hollywood. They could be in Rome. They could be in London. They're the cream of television talent. And all they're doing is sitting around on their high-priced butts drinking tea, just because they haven't had your scripts.'

'My word,' said Henry.

'I want you to come and meet Brad,' said Jocelyn Pride. 'He's the script editor. He'll get your script camera-ready, so don't worry about cuts or close ups or anything like that. Just tell us a simple moving story. Brad, this is Henry the author.'

Brad sat staring into the screen of the word-processor on his desk and said nothing.

'How are the rewrites going, Brad?' asked Pride.

Brad silently scrolled a good few pages of text through the little screen in front of him.

'The rewrites?' said Henry. 'But how can he be doing the rewrites? I haven't even done the writes yet.'

'Lord Mellow wants the rewrites done first on this project,' said Jocelyn Pride. 'We've really got to speed things up if we're going to film in the autumn and screen in the spring. You can trust Brad. He doesn't say much, but his written dialogue is great.'

'Joss, Streep isn't available,' said a girl in a Colorado ski-team sweatshirt, putting down her telephone at the next desk.

'You win some and you lose some,' said Jocelyn Pride. 'Lord Mellow particularly wanted Meryl Streep. This is Gill, the casting director. Meet Henry, who wrote the script.'

'Who's still writing it,' said Henry.

'Great,' said Gill, opening up an enormously fat book on her desk that was called *Spotlight*. 'Can I just check out some of the casting with you?'

'I don't see how we can even think about casting, if it hasn't been written yet,' said Henry.

'Do you know how long in advance you have to book leading actors?' said Gill. 'We're late already. That's how we lost Streep. But how about her for the role?'

Gill showed Henry a photograph of a very beautiful girl of around twenty-five, who wore a low-cut dress and pouted at the camera. Next to the photograph was the name Jonquil Pouvoir.

'She certainly looks attractive,' said Henry.

'Well, she doesn't quite look like that *now*,' said Gill. 'The photograph must be ten years old and I'm not sure it's her anyway. And she's got fat since the mastectomy. But she's available for the whole four-month shoot and she's ideal for the part.'

74

'What part?' asked Henry.

'The Streep part,' said Gill. 'The main part. Any part. So long as it's female. Oh, and this is really great news. We've got Sir Luke Trimingham.'

'Who?' asked Henry.

'The acting knight, that's who,' said Gill. 'Lord Mellow offered him an open account at Berry Brothers and Rudd and he accepted like a lamb. He says he wants to die in the final scene.'

'I haven't written the final scene,' said Henry. 'Or anywhere near it.'

'That should make things easier,' said Pride.

'I don't like writing dying in my work,' said Henry. 'I'm quite superstitious about it.'

'But it's written into Sir Luke's contract,' said Gill. 'All the other acting knights have had big memorable dying scenes in series lately and Sir Luke wants to get one. He wants to die in bed with his mouth open.'

'I'm not sure it's consistent with my concept . . .' began Henry, but Jocelyn Pride seized him by the arm and led him through more and more desks until they came to a small private office at the end of the room.

'Let's go in here,' said Pride. 'I want you to meet Roger Trothammer, the prod. ass.'

'What's a prod. ass.?' asked Henry.

'Just the lynchpin of the entire production, that's all,' said Pride. 'Especially now Lord Mellow has made himself executive producer. He plans the production, works out the budget, organises resources, he does everything.'

Roger Trothammer sat behind the desk in his little office, in front of a wall covered with coloured flow charts. He had telephones to both ears which he put down as Henry and Pride came in.

'This is our writer, Henry Babbacombe,' said Pride. 'He's brought us some scripts.'

'How very generous and thoughtful of him,' said Roger Trothammer, looking at Henry with what he could not but feel was a malign expression. 'I hope it doesn't ruin the production. Things have been going quite well up to now. I hope you told him about the big production meeting this morning?'

'There hasn't been time,' said Pride.

'Some very fundamental decisions had to be taken,' said Roger Trothammer. 'It's only two months to first day of principal photography.'

'Andrew Lloyd Webber's doing the music,' said Pride.

'I fixed that,' said Roger Trothammer.

'Mark Hasper's going to direct,' said Pride.

'I fixed that,' said Roger Trothammer. 'We flew him in from Hollywood this morning.'

'You'll meet him at dinner this evening at the Roaring Bullock,' said Jocelyn Pride. 'Rog and Brad and Gill will be there, and Cyn – she's dying to see you again. Have we got you a hotel?'

'Yes,' said Roger Trothammer, 'I fixed that.'

'You don't think we're rushing things a bit?' asked Henry.

'Jesus, writers!' said Roger Trothammer. 'Do you have any idea what it takes to mount a major television series? We have to book the planes, book the hotels, hire twenty vans and generators, schedule fifty people for different periods in locations all over Japan ...'

'We have to plan the shooting schedule, know who's where doing what when for every day of a four-month shoot, we have to provide them with food, we have to provide them with portable toilet facilities . . .' said Pride.

'Did you say Japan?' asked Henry.

'We're locating the story in Japan,' said Pride. 'Lord Mellow's arranged a fabulous co-production deal there, with full technical facilities included.'

'Lord Mellow!' said Roger Trothammer. 'I fixed that.'

'But I don't know anything about Japan,' said Henry. 'I don't know anything at all about it. I can't even remember where it is.'

'Okay, we'll hire you a researcher, two researchers,' said Roger Trothammer. 'I'll just write myself a note reminding me to fix it.'

'He's a brilliant man, and totally ruthless,' said Pride approvingly as they left the office. 'He's given you a really prestigious production.'

'I somehow felt he didn't like me very much,' said Henry.

'That's because you were chosen as writer before he came on to the project,' said Pride, 'so he didn't fix that. Rog is fine if you just stand up to him. Now, I should get you over to your hotel. It's right across the street. Take a shower, wash off the sheep, and join us at the Roaring Bullock at eight. I'll send a driver to pick you up.'

A little later on, Henry Babbacombe stood in the shower in the pleasant little suite at the hotel across the road, and knew he had not really cut much of a figure that afternoon. There were writers, and there were television writers; he seemed hardly cut out to be one of the second kind. Indeed, as he got out of the shower and saw his bare white body reflected back at him from the steamy bathroom mirror, he realised he did not cut much of a figure at all. His white fleshy substance, so little used, so given over to thought, so unhabituated to life, looked like a great blank sheet of paper on which everything had yet to be written: in this exactly resembling his script.

He went through into the bedroom of the little suite, where someone had left a kettle, sachets of coffee, and a bottle of Mouton Cadet in a bucket of smoking ice. Henry poured some of the wine, which seemed very pleasant, into a glass, took his script from his briefcase, lay down on the bed and began to read. In the offices at Eldorado, which flashed at him through the window, they were doubtless doing the same. The script, with its mad cuts and cutaways, its moody moods and atmospheric atmospheres, suddenly seemed absurd in the light of what it was to occasion: round-the-world airline tickets and travelling trucks, expensive directors and famous actors, location catering and portable toilets, the true stuff of television drama. Beside the bed was a little electronic raygun, and Henry picked it up. Some little doors in the wall opened, and a television set was revealed. It flared into life, and there was the Eldorado television news. The Tory lead had been cut in the polls. This was likely to lead to cuts in taxes and rates. There might be deep cuts in nuclear arms. Henry pressed a button; Botham was cutting a ball to the boundary. Henry yawned and looked at the clock in the bedside console. The doubtless traumatic meeting at the Roaring Bullock was still two hours off. His sleepless night, his dreadful day, and the experience of reading his own script had made him very tired. There was certainly time for a little nap, and Henry, in the flickering light of the television set, let his eyes slide shut.

9

At a very big table at the rear of the Roaring Bullock, the elegant gourmet restaurant that some cunning architect had managed to refurbish from part of what had once been the city abattoir, the party from Eldorado had already got things cut and dried.

Henry arrived late, half an hour late; the nap had turned into a sleep, and only the experienced reaction of the driver, used, as it proved, to the ways of authors, who had called several times from the lobby until he had roused him, had got him there at all. At the Roaring Bullock, the waiters wore Breton fishing sweaters and big black berets, and were evidently very friendly, shouting pleasant endearments at him as he followed the table hostess, who wore a low-cut dress with a high slit in its skirt, down the room. A monocled pianist played selections from Piaf, and there were Bouguereau paintings on the walls. It was clearly a high-class sort of place, but in television one evidently lived quite well.

The party from Eldorado had clearly been there for some time already, if the empty aperitif glasses and the dozen or so bottles in front of them were any kind of guide. Joss and Brad, Rog and Gill, sat there, each holding a glass in one hand and a copy of Henry's script in the other. Then there was a small middle-aged man with a leather jerkin, metal-rimmed spectacles and a small chin-beard, who was being treated with considerable respect and being told lots of stories. They all looked up coldly at Henry.

But Cynthia Hyde-Lemon was at the head of the table, and as Jocelyn Pride had promised, she seemed very pleased to see him. 'Oh, Henry,' she said, rising, kissing him very fulsomely on both his cheeks, and squeezing his right buttock with some force, 'we've had such a good talk about your script. Do meet Mark Hasper, our director. We've just flown him in from Hollywood. He's one of the best in the business.'

'The best in the business,' said Roger Trothammer.

'And Henry is our writer,' said Cynthia Hyde-Lemon.

Mark Hasper cast his metal-framed spectacles up and down Henry and said, 'The writer, hey? Nice to have met you.'

'I asked him to join us,' said Cynthia. 'I thought it would be amusing. Get a glass from the next table, Henry. We're just tasting a rather nice Saint Julien Mark said was rather moreish.'

Roger Trothammer ordered another six bottles, so that they could taste it even better, and then the crowd at the table stopped looking at Henry and began telling each other interesting stories about various shoots they had been on. There were shoots where all the crew, of both sexes, had attempted to seduce the leading lady, and shoots where the leading lady had attempted to seduce all the crew; shoots where the director had been eaten by piranha fish, and shoots where piranha fish had been eaten by the director. It was not until later, over the quenelles de brochette with kiwi fruit, that anyone referred to Henry's script.

'Maybe we should just talk about Henry's script,' said Jocelyn Pride, as Roger Trothammer ordered another six bottles of the Saint Julien.

Mark Hasper, who had a rather severe look, said, 'But

the writer's here.'

'Lord Mellow has this philosophy of always respecting the writer,' said Cynthia Hyde-Lemon. 'He mentioned it once at the Edinburgh Festival and now he's stuck with it.'

'That's right,' said Jocelyn Pride, in his brown suit. 'Henry, we've all seen your script and we've read it with care and discussed it in detail. We thought it was great, Henry.'

'You did?' said Henry.

'Really great,' said Cynthia Hyde-Lemon.

'You didn't think it was a bit too maroon?' asked Henry.

'No, we all read it with care and we thought it was really great,' said Jocelyn Pride.

'That's wonderful,' said Henry.

'However,' said Mark Hasper, 'and in television there is always a however, we thought there were just a few problems.'

'For instance,' said Roger Trothammer, 'for thirteen hours of television it is a little short.'

'That's right. At a rough guess, without doing an exact timing on it, I'd say it was about twelve hours forty-five minutes too short,' said Mark Hasper. 'But that's only a rough guess.'

'We realise you *intended* it to be short,' said Cynthia, 'but even for short it's really very short.'

'But that's just a sort of an attempt at the opening,' said Henry. 'I just wanted to establish the basic atmosphere.'

'Something tells me atmosphere is very important to you, Henry,' said Mark Hasper.

'That's right,' said Henry.

81

'That's why you write such a lot of it?' asked Mark
Hasper.

'I suppose I do,' said Henry.

'An atmosphere of indescribable menace,' said Roger
Trothammer.

'Of unbearable tension,' said Jocelyn Pride.

'Of erotic anticipation,' said Cynthia Hyde-Lemon.

'In fact, Henry, very few writers can portray atmosphere in quite the way you do,' said Mark Hasper. 'It's
fantastic. But may I just check something? You do write
dialogue as well?'

'Oh, yes,' said Henry, 'There'll be a lot of that later,
once we've established the atmosphere.'

'And characters?' asked Roger Trothammer. 'I mean,
characters with names? And motivations?'

'And plots?' asked Mark Hasper. 'Do you do plots at
all? I just want to get the picture.'

'Oh, yes,' said Henry, 'I do all that.'

'Climaxes?' asked Cynthia Hyde-Lemon.

'Climaxes are actually my main problem,' admitted
Henry. 'I do have trouble getting to my climaxes.'

'Do you really, Henry?' said Cynthia Hyde-Lemon.

'Great,' said Mark Hasper, filling up the glasses. 'That's
great. Henry, I wonder whether you've ever noticed that
television scripts have very wide margins?'

'Yes, I know,' said Henry. 'I read a book about it.'

'Do you know *why* they have wide margins?' asked
Mark Hasper.

'No,' said Henry.

'I'll tell you, Henry,' said Mark Hasper. 'They have
wide margins so that people can write in those margins.
Do you mind if, out of our television experience, we just
write a few small things in the margins of yours?'

'Not at all,' said Henry. 'I'm always very receptive to suggestions.'

'Are you really, Henry?' said Cynthia Hyde-Lemon.

'That's great,' said Mark Hasper, 'really great. Because we have just one or two. Nothing of course that changes the essential concept. Just a few things that might fill out the story and actually give us thirteen hours of television time, without which, quite frankly, Henry, we are going to be screwed, really screwed. Thirteen hours of television is really a very long time, Henry. We are asking people to give us thirteen hours of their lives, to stop their cooking, to quit their love-making, to stay at home when they could be mugging old ladies in the street, to switch over from *Dallas*, to burn electrical current at high prices, we are asking them to do that, and we want to make it worth their while. That's the only reason we're making these suggestions, Henry. May we put them to you?'

'Oh, do,' said Henry.

'Brad,' said Mark Hasper.

Brad, who had spent most of the meal so far nose down in the *cuisine minceur*, suddenly proved articulate.

'Well, here are just a few reactions I had after reading your very fine script,' said Brad.

'Very fine script,' said Mark Hasper.

'I saw it as essentially a story about this love affair between a very attractive Englishwoman with mysterious eyes, and this Japanese samurai from one of Japan's great families, who meet in the 1930s under the shadow of impending war.'

'That was my reaction too,' said Jocelyn Pride.

'In the lovely city of Kyoto, a place of temple bells and shrines, they meet by chance in a teahouse and at once they fall in love,' said Brad.

83

'That's a very beautiful location, and one I can work with,' said Mark Hasper.

'They have a very tempestuous relationship and then they're ...'

'Separated,' said Cynthia Hyde-Lemon.

'By the war, and because she cannot understand his Shinto faith. She comes home to Britain, and a child is born,' said Brad.

'A child is born,' said Cynthia. 'That would make an alternative title.'

'The child is a girl, and as she grows into adult life ...'

'This could be the Jonquil Pouvoir part,' said Gill.

'... she decides to hunt for both her parents, from whom she has been ...'

'Separated,' said Cynthia Hyde-Lemon, beginning to cry.

'... by a strange quirk of fate. She looks for her mother, who had sent her away because back in Britain during the war she is wooed and won by a very rich British lord with a beautiful country estate.'

'You know who could play that?' cried Gill. 'Sir Luke Trimingham!'

'She finds her mother, and they are ...'

'Reunited,' wept Cynthia Hyde-Lemon.

'Her mother sends her off to Japan to find her father. He has been a wartime hero and now he's the head of a great Japanese corporation. He's now married to a beautiful geisha. In the grounds of a temple they meet and are ...'

'Reunited,' sobbed Cynthia Hyde-Lemon.

'He takes her to his fabulous house, and there she meets her Japanese cousin, a great inventor. The girl and her cousin fall in love. They climb Mount Fuji together.

Alas, they are ...'

'Separated,' cried Cynthia Hyde-Lemon, her make-up running terribly.

'News has come of a family tragedy. In his ancient fourposter bed on the great estate, the old lord is now breathing his last ...'

'Sir Luke could play that beautifully,' said Gill.

'But as he lies on his deathbed he suddenly remembers a young man who had saved his life in a Japanese prison camp after he had been sentenced to be beheaded. He wants the young man to be chairman of his great chain of companies. The young man is sent for, and by the deathbed ...'

'It's a very long deathbed,' said Mark Hasper.

'He sees a weeping girl. The young man is the Japanese cousin!'

'Wonderful,' said Jocelyn Pride.

'So, brought together by the wise old lord, the two get together again. They inherit the estate. They take over the corporation.'

'They invent the Honda Accord,' said Cynthia Hyde-Lemon.

'They marry in the ancient chapel on the estate. The old samurai comes to the ceremony. His wife has died. As they stand in the glorious chapel, he looks across at the girl's mother, his one true love. They look at each other and are ...'

'Reunited,' cried Cynthia Hyde-Lemon, sobbing loudly. 'It's beautiful. Fantastic. Brilliant, Henry. Congratulations.'

'I knew you'd write us a great script,' said Jocelyn Pride. Just then a waiter in a beret came, put his arm round him, and whispered in his ear.

'There's a telephone call for me,' said Pride, rising. 'But do go on discussing Henry's great script.'

Henry sat and thought.

'You don't think it's a bit banal and conventional?' he asked.

'Henry, ask yourself, why do conventions exist?' said Mark Hasper. 'They exist because people need them and love them and understand them. They don't want surprises. They don't want unfamiliar stories.'

'They don't want unknown foreign languages,' said Roger Trothammer.

'They want clear motives with strong muscles,' said Cynthia.

'I feel it could be missing something,' said Henry. 'Some element of experimentalism, some sense of surprise, some ... difference.'

'Henry,' said Roger Trothammer, 'Eldorado is not an experimental company. Our people don't go to Cannes. They don't give lectures at the ICA on the frontiers of television drama. They look for what people like, and they give it to them. That's the Eldorado way.'

'It's got everything,' said Cynthia Hyde-Lemon. 'Past and present, then and now.'

'Love and feeling, ancient buildings and contemporary problems,' said Roger Trothammer.

'Terrific casting potential,' said Gill.

'Great foreign locations,' said Roger Trothammer.

'An international dimension that will sell it in America, and I don't mean to PBS,' said Mark Hasper.

'It's got everything,' said Cynthia Hyde-Lemon, 'except a ukelele. Can't we just work in one little ukelele?'

Just then Jocelyn Pride came back.

'That was Lord Mellow,' he said. 'I told him about your

script, Henry. He thinks it's great, really great.'

'That's great,' said Cynthia.

'There's just one problem,' said Pride. 'The Japanese deal is off. Lord Mellow's sewn up this absolutely fantastic co-production deal with the Swiss. They want it shot in the Alps.'

'But that's not where I set my story,' said Henry. 'I couldn't change my script, not just like that. I set it in Japan.'

'Of course you did, Henry,' said Cynthia Hyde-Lemon, squeezing his leg under the table, 'but it just means more rewrites. We'll help you, Henry.'

'We're real professionals,' said Mark Hasper.

'So why don't you just stick around for a few days,' said Cynthia, as Roger Trothammer ordered more wine.

The next morning Henry woke in the unfamiliar hotel room with an unfamiliar headache. For some reason he had failed to put on his pyjamas. He felt round in the bed for them, and discovered something else very unfamiliar, a very large and very naked body that was lying snugly beside him.

'Henry,' said Cynthia Hyde-Lemon, sitting up without any sign of her boilersuit, 'and how are you today?'

'I'm not sure,' said Henry. 'My script. What did they do to my script?'

'Forget the script,' said Cynthia, and her hands came toward him under the duvet. 'Put it in the wastepaper basket. Flush it down the loo. Save it for your posthumous collected works. It's done its job.'

'I don't think I'm a television writer at all,' said Henry, staring desperately up at the ceiling. 'I don't understand how I ever got the job.'

'Joss Pride was sleeping that week with the girl called

Kenneth,' said Cynthia. 'He promised to take someone from her agency, and the only one she could come up with was you.'

'I'll never make it,' said Henry. 'I could never write that story.'

'Come on, Henry,' said Cynthia, who was for some reason now on top of him, 'we're very professional people. Just put yourself entirely in our hands. This problem you have with your climaxes, for example. We can fix that.'

And so, as it proved, she could; and Henry decided after all to stick around for a few days, as Cynthia suggested, and put himself entirely in her very professional hands.

10

So, over the few brief weeks that followed, the great team that had been gathered to produce *Serious Damage* worked and worked to cut and hew Henry's struggling little script into shape.

The days went by, the summer of 1986 became the wet, windy autumn, the 1980s moved a bit closer toward becoming the 1990s, the twentieth century shuddered on the edge of becoming the twenty-first, the second Christian millennium moved with an appropriate sense of apocalypse towards its last and final days, and the first day of principal photography grew ever nearer on the series that was to be shot in the autumn and shown in the spring. On the television screens that flickered and flared in all the offices at Eldorado another endless, abrasive, banal serial showed daily, the seamless, ever-unrolling tale of misery, violence, despair, obscenity, greed and conflict that is called the news. Faces shone out of the sets, faces of people competing for money competing with people for power in an endless competition for fame. There were trials and heart-transplants, riots and bomb-blasts. At Chernobyl a Russian nuclear reactor erupted and sent its lethal radiation across most of Northern Europe. Industrial pollution poured down the major rivers and corrupted the seas. Acid rain deforested the hillsides, and car exhaust emissions were burning off the protective ozone layer. AIDS was spreading epidemically, along with cervical cancer, meningitis and innumerable untreatable viruses. Famine was growing, drought and desolation multiplying, small wars erupting, and terror was coming out of the always fundamentalist Middle East to threaten the newly fundamentalist West. Manufacturing industry was declining, jobs for the young were disappearing, financial speculation was increasing, and everyone was waiting for the Big Bang. Rape and child-murder were increasing, crime-figures escalating, the centres of great cities deteriorating. Sex was lethal, smoking abhorrent, drinking dangerous, food destructive, and indeed the only pleasure left to make life worth living, if it was at all, was money, poor little paper money, which was trying to do all the work. It was a serial that Henry watched intermittently, glancing at its banal horrors, its bland tragedies, its half-apocalyptic messages, its unstructured and chaotic plots. It made him glad to be writing a serial of his own, shapely, ordered and elegant. It even made him understand why people might actually want to watch a tale of reassuring characters, traditional and solid houses, established customs, sunlit lawns, sentimental feelings, flowing nostalgia and an all too happy ending – the sort of tale that somehow, as he worked along with the team at Eldorado, *Serious Damage* was showing every sign of becoming.

For writing for television was teamwork, and Henry had even moved now from the safe village across the moors – leaving the little garden shed to neglect and the field-mice – to the great sad city. The idea was Lord Mellow's, and he pursued it insistently. Henry had not taken to it at first, fearful that he would be cutting himself off from his roots, cutting himself off from his art. Yet in the end Lord Mellow's advice proved sound. The news that he was writing a major television series had spread quickly through the village community, like one of the many epidemics that now filled the newsreels, and it had not won him the respect he might have supposed. People who had simply ignored Henry for years now went out of their way to cut him dead, whether because they blamed him for the abysmal summer scheduling or were envious of his new-found fame it was hard to say. But somehow he had become a stranger in the village. And he had been unwise enough to grant a second interview to the girl from Radio Haywain, who had learned some technology in the meantime, so the local airwaves were filled with Henry boasting of the intimate relationship he now enjoyed with the likes of Sir Luke Trimingham and Jonquil Pouvoir, neither of whom he had yet met. This too had not gone down well, and produced unfortunate consequences: the following morning Mrs Raper, on whom so much depended, had turned up in distress with her notice. For her Jack had found, in what she called one of the steroids, an article by Jonquil Pouvoir giving a very detailed account of some of the famous parts she had had. 'And I don't mean acting parts either, Mr Babbacombe,' Mrs Raper had said. 'These was human parts. Parts of some very big people, very big people indeed. So Jack says I mustn't enter your den of permisscuity ever again.'

Henry therefore thought it best to fall in with Lord Mellow's advice, and it was probably as well, for in due time he came to realise that he would never have become professional enough to finish the series without it. For, as Lord Mellow kept insisting, up there in his high office, television is a collaborative medium, made out of many inputs and outputs. So Roger Trothammer grudgingly found Henry a tiny desk in a dark corner of the great office at Eldorado, and somewhat unwillingly booked him a much smaller suite in the hotel just across the road. This meant that for the first time Henry was able to attend all the script conferences and storyline development workshops, casting sessions and production meetings, necessary lunchtime drinks in pubs and obligatory late meals in expensive restaurants that making a major television project is all about. He realised that his presence was quite indispensable, or at least no more dispensable than anyone else's. Here he began to learn the arts of collaboration and compromise, the pleasures and pains of working with a brilliant, well-oiled, indeed often extremely well-oiled team, and the wisdom of putting himself in professional hands. He decided it made sense to stay on in the great sad city, until the fuss in the village had subsided, the decisions about the project made, the thirteen scripts finished, the job done, and the time came to return to something resembling real life again.

If, that is, the scripts ever were to be finished. In his weaker moments, Henry decided the task was impossible. He wrote, of course; indeed he wrote and wrote and wrote. He wrote by day, in the office in the glass tower; he wrote by night, on the dressing table in the hotel suite across the street. He wrote as he ate, he ate as he wrote. Scenes and acts and episodes began scrolling out of the battered roller of the old Remington portable; reams of paper stacked up on his desk. What he wrote he passed on to Brad, who rewrote it and handed it to Pride, who rewrote it and handed it on to one of Mark Hasper's several secretaries, who rewrote it and sent it back to Henry to be rewritten. For television was indeed, as Lord

Mellow said, a collaborative medium, and nothing was really written, but rewritten. Nothing held stable, nothing stayed the same, as it did with novels. The Japanese samurai had somehow become an old Scots ghillie. The great country house had somehow become a castle on a foreign lake. New ideas came from nowhere, had their time, then ended up back in nowhere.

Meanwhile the rest of the production team kept busy. A man was hired who just worked on the year 1936. Mark Hasper himself was proving somewhat elusive, shutting himself in his vast curtained office for casting sessions, staying in expensive foreign hotels looking over locations, going off to cottages in the Cotswolds to work on his camera script or rehearsing actors in small church halls in depressing areas of the city in front of piles of chairs that were described to them as the Swiss Alps. But he now had three assistant directors who came to Henry's desk with his messages, each one of them claiming in different and opposite ways to know the contents of his mind. At first Henry found this dismaying, until he gradually came to understand how they worked. Thus, if Henry wrote down the script instruction 'night', they changed it to 'day'. If he wrote 'sunlight', they simply altered it to 'rain'. If he wrote 'interior', they crossed it out and wrote 'exterior'. If he put the word 'London', they pencilled it through and scribbled 'Paris'. If he wrote a scene that ran for ten minutes they cut it down to one that lasted for fifteen seconds. If he wrote a scene that lasted for fifteen seconds they invented something visual that lasted for ten minutes. If he put a dramatic event at the end of one episode, professional instinct told them to remove it and place it at the beginning of another. Henry gathered after a while that it did not really matter what he wrote, so long as he wrote something someone else could find a way to change. He also gathered that he could get exactly what he wanted, simply by writing down the opposite. If he wanted something on film – and he was learning all about film – he wrote down 'videotape'. If he wanted something done on location – and he was learning all about locations – he wrote down 'studio'. He also understood that everyone else was there to change everything else that everyone else did. When Mark Hasper made him write a scene that was expensive, Roger Trothammer came and made him write a scene that was cheap. Versions multiplied, variants burgeoned, and Henry's was not one script but several. In fact, now that he had put himself into professional hands, Henry knew he was becoming quite professional himself.

But no hands were more pleasing or more professional than those of Cynthia Hyde-Lemon, and he resorted to them often. Indeed one of the main reasons Henry stayed in the great sad city was that it facilitated regular proximity to her. It was not that they ever had much time together; after all, Cynthia was a busy executive lady with a full appointments book. But Henry's hotel was conveniently across the street from the Eldorado tower, and at many various and irregular hours of day or night – Henry soon lost touch with which was which – she would tap on the door of Henry's suite, already unzipping her latest boiler suit, to use some small gap in her diary to its best advantage. These brief sessions were always well spent, and so was Henry afterwards. She would snatch the pile of scripts from the dressing table as she cast off her clothes and headed for the bed, meanwhile chattering in a barrage of professional jargon of peaks and troughs, cliffhangers and breaks, a jargon that itself seemed to confuse Aristotle's *Poetics* with passages from the *Kamasutra*. Indeed when he thought about it afterwards, Henry found it as difficult to disentangle her wise advice, so very different in character from Professor Finniston's, as it was for them to disentangle themselves from each other at the end of these brief visits. What was sex and what was art? What was bed and what was typewriter?

'Let's take a look at this muscle here,' Cynthia would say, as they lay naked on the bed in a pile of paper. 'It's just not tight enough, is it?'

'In the script?' asked Henry.

'In the script, Henry,' said Cynthia. 'Look, put your opening here, put in some tension there, and this is where your end ought to be, right?'

'In the script?' asked Henry.

'In the script, Henry, in the script,' said Cynthia. 'Now we want the top here and the tail there. And let's forget the foreplay and get straight to the climax.'

'In the script?' asked Henry.

'Jesus, no,' said Cynthia. 'Get to it, Henry. I've got a production meeting with Lord Mellow in ten minutes.'

So Cynthia would come, as would he, and Cynthia would go; and he would stay, picking up from the crumpled sheets the crumpled sheets, and sit down at the little typewriter, banging the keys with a fresh sense of tension and conflict, act and episode. In later years Henry would realise how much he had learned about life, and art, and the confusion between the two, in the tiny hotel bedroom. And there was no doubt that if the blank page of both his script and his being was now being filled with writing, then that was all very much due to Cyn.

Then one day it was all done, and five typists with five typewriters worked through five nights to type and print and bind and stack the great pile of thirteen scripts in their revised final version, which said *Serious Damage* on the cover and had Henry's name in quite big letters underneath. There were acting scripts and shooting scripts, and schedules and cast-lists, to add to the great pile, the sum of the work that had been done in the great office and completed just in time. Henry leafed through the great stack that rose up toward the ceiling, not just a work of art but instructions for four months of production, the employment of hundreds of people, the expenditure of millions of pounds. It was true that the work was not quite in Henry's usual style, which had been described as 'obscure but glittering with wit' (*Daily Telegraph*), 'busty and bouncy with Beckettian overtones' (*Daily Mail*) and 'paradigmatically intertextual and parodically postmodern' (*Glyph*). If Henry's work had been famous, albeit among a tiny elite of well-chosen readers, for its self-referential and self-conscious textuality, a Structuralist critic could work away on this for ten years and find no sign of signifier or the stuff. Where his previous art had been noticed, by the happy few who notice such things, for its hard ironies and its refusal of the concept of character, in the manner of Samuel Beckett, this long and moving tale of two generations of lovers was of a somewhat different calibre, and rather resembled Elinor Glyn at her uckiest. And if it so happened that a maroon quality was what you were looking for, well, you could read these several thousand pages and find nothing maroon about them at all.

But at least there were thirteen episodes, each on different-coloured paper. There was a story that should reach not a thousand readers but many millions. There was love and power and tenderness and glory, and a lot of mountains in the background. The scenes were short, the muscles were tight, the climaxes were climactic. The scripts had come out long enough; Mark Hasper and his timing team had testified to it. They had come out within the programme budget; Roger Trothammer, grudgingly, had admitted as much. They had proper parts for actors to play and were consistent with the casting; Gill had said so. They were filmable in a reasonable shooting sequence; Brad had ensured it. They matched the schedule of locations; the location finder had called up from somewhere on Corfu to affirm it. They had dramatic conflict and sound cliffhangers; Cyn said so. They had nice little holes in the middle of the story for advertisements; Jocelyn Pride had made sure of it. And they had made it in time, just in time for everyone to have them before the series party that Lord Mellow was to give in his penthouse suite at the top of the glass tower on the Friday before the last vans left, the cast got in their transportation and went to Heathrow, the cameras were loaded and shooting was started in Switzerland on the following Monday.

Henry went back to his room and got ready for the party; he even, gambling on future profits, went out into the city and bought himself an expensive tie for the event. That evening he stood inside the glass lift in the Eldorado tower as it ascended the vast atrium in the general direction of Lord Mellow's suite. The lift was crowded with people Henry did not recognise; he assumed them to be actors, the actors who had been stranded out in their remote church halls rehearsing and so kept well out of sight. But if they were actors they seemed strangely subdued and quiet, somehow lacking in their natural flamboyance. In fact, with his famous sensitivity to such matters, he detected an atmosphere of something. Could it be sinister unease? Or baffled anticipation? Henry was not sure as he followed them out of the vertiginous lift and over to the white doors that led to Lord Mellow's high penthouse.

He went in to the great room over the city, the lights of which flickered and flashed far down below. There they all were, the people he had been working with for months – Cyn and Joss, Roger and Brad, Gill and Mark, the three assistant directors, the designers, the costumes people, the camera team, the dressers, the casting people, a big girl in kneewarmers who never seemed to do anything very much, the man who was the expert on the year 1936. Besides the people he had seen before there were many he had not seen before: the actors, some new technicians, the Head of Finance, the Head of Technical Staff. Big cars had brought big men, the members of the Board, in from their broad acres in the shires; Lord Lenticule was there, inconveniently asleep in a chair right in front of the canapés. Caterers from GNOSH went around with drinks and bits, but something of the same odd atmosphere that had prevailed in the lift seemed to be there in the room as well. Everyone was decidedly quiet and many were drinking far too much, even for them. What was it? Erotic anxiety? Indescribable menace? Cynthia Hyde-Lemon stood in a corner talking very nervously with the first and second assistant directors. Mark Hasper sat in a chair with his head in his hands, then suddenly got up and asked to be taken to a telephone. A strained-looking and dank-haired lady of about fifty stood in a low-cut dress in the middle of the room, accompanied by a man with silver-grey hair and a very expensive suit; she seemed to be crying quite loudly.

'Who's the batty lady over there?' Henry asked the big girl in kneewarmers, who had always appeared friendly, 'the one with the grey-haired man?'

'Don't you recognise her?' asked the girl. 'That's just the star of the show, Jonquil Pouvoir. And the man with her's her personal psychiatrist. God, I don't think I've been to a party this gloomy since the day they gave the boot to *Gladstone, Man of Empire*.'

'What was that?' asked Henry.

'Just Eldorado's last big serial, that's all,' said the girl.

'They gave it the boot?' said Henry.

''Chopped it, cut it, axed it, cancelled it,' said the girl.

'Did they?' said Henry.

'And not just that,' said the girl. 'They tore it up, they shredded it, they pulped it.'

'Well, they wouldn't do that to this, not now,' said Henry.

'Wouldn't they?' said the girl. 'Why isn't Lord Mellow here, then?'

'Why isn't Lord Mellow here, then?' said Henry, going over to Cynthia Hyde-Lemon, who was still in the corner in a maroon boilersuit with the first and second assistant directors.

'Maybe he doesn't like that stuff you wrote,' said Cynthia in what seemed a rather cool way.

'We wrote,' said Henry.

'You wrote,' said Cynthia.

'Could he cancel it?' asked Henry.

'The whole project can't move without his go-ahead,

and he hasn't come to give it,' said Cynthia. 'Mark thinks he'll cancel. He's already on the phone to Hollywood looking for a new project with Robert Redford. He says there are some very nasty signs.'

'What signs?' asked Henry.

'Sir Luke Trimingham didn't turn up to rehearsals,' said Cynthia. 'And he and Lord Mellow spend a lot of time together on the golfcourse these days.'

'But they've spent so much money on it,' said Henry, going white. 'All this team of brilliant people. The vans are driving to Switzerland. All the hotels are booked.'

'He could just write it off to experience,' said Cynthia. 'We've all had a lot of experience. Especially you, Henry.'

'I have, it's true,' said Henry.

'And speaking of that, give me your room-key, would you?' murmured Cynthia. 'I've left something I need in your bathroom.'

As Henry glanced round, then handed over his key, there was a great wind and a thunderous battering on the windows of the penthouse suite. Everyone turned and stared. Lord Mellow's helicopter flew by, and a moment later it landed on the roof.

'Oh, Jesus,' said Cynthia Hyde-Lemon, and the room went silent. Even the caterers stopped catering.

Then, after a few minutes, the doors to Lord Mellow's suite opened, and he came out, still wearing his helmet. He was accompanied by Sir Luke Trimingham, in his Burberry coat and scarf. Lord Mellow looked round, took off his helmet, and walked straight across the room to Henry.

'Aren't you the young man who wrote this?' he asked. 'Come and meet Sir Luke Trimingham. He's been reading your scripts.'

People stopped talking and turned to stare as Lord Mellow seized Henry by the arm and led him across the room to the great acting knight, who looked Henry up and down.

'My word, so you are the young fellow who is the *fons et origo* of the present farrago,' said Sir Luke in his famous tones. 'Well, it is always fascinating to meet an author. They are always so remarkably disappointing. However, perhaps even the Great Bard himself was no wow at a party.'

'I don't think we know,' said Henry.

'Sir Luke has some reflections on your script,' said Lord Mellow.

People crowded round and there was an atmosphere of total silence.

'Yes, I read it,' said Sir Luke. 'On a beastly jumbo from the United States. It's quite awful, isn't it?'

'The flight?' said Henry hopefully.

'No, your script,' said Sir Luke Trimingham. 'A completely untalented piece of hackery, a purely mechanical artifact without any quality or any substance. A tissue of faked emotion and falsified eloquence. Entirely lacking in moral truth, or any kind of real human seriousness. Utterly failing to extend the medium or advance the possibilities of our dramatic arts by the slightest jot or tittle. Confirming the viewer in the most banal sentiments. Flattering him in his folly, his vanity, his vulgar nostalgia, his natural avarice, his barbaric cynicism. Oh, yes, I liked it greatly.'

'He liked it,' said Lord Mellow.

'You liked it?' said Mark Hasper, who had come back from the telephone, in incredulity.

People began to laugh and kiss each other.

'Particularly that extraordinarily banal and totally spurious death-scene at the end,' said Sir Luke. 'I do believe I shall be able to play that quite beautifully.'

'So you are happy to play in it?' asked Mark Hasper.

'Dear boy, I expect to play in it,' said Sir Luke. 'In fact I thought that settled long ago. That is why our advocates invented that great British institution, the binding contract. I trust you intend to honour it, Mellow: I have already ordered very large quantities of some very fine wines.'

'Of course,' said Lord Mellow hastily.

'But you didn't come to rehearsals,' said Mark Hasper.

'Didn't they tell you, dear boy?' said Sir Luke. 'I never come to rehearsals. I know exactly what I shall do already. I should be very foolish to let other people see it in advance. They might improve their acting, and we don't want that.'

'Excellent,' said Lord Mellow. 'We just wondered whether you might have baulked at ...'

'The ukelele?' said Sir Luke. 'A singularly felicitous touch.'

'I didn't put in a ukelele,' said Henry.

'In episode seven,' said Sir Luke. 'Most people never think of looking there. That is why I always read episode seven first.'

'If you didn't, who did?' asked Lord Mellow.

Everyone looked round for Cynthia Hyde-Lemon, but she was gone. And so were the first and second assistant directors, a crate of wine, and Henry's room-key.

'Then a toast!' said Lord Mellow, climbing on to the top of his white desk. 'To *Serious Damage!*'

People raised their glasses and kissed each other some more. Even Lord Lenticule woke up.

102

'To a good shoot and a balanced budget,' cried Lord Mellow, and the glasses all went up. 'To a well-kept schedule and everything in on time. To many prizes and hundreds of residuals. To fame and fortune. To the renewal of our contract. To our fine stars and our talented designers. To our gifted author, Harold Pinter. My friends, I think I know a winner when I see one, and I see one now. This is a story that has everything. Love and power. Past and present. Tears and laughter. Sense and sensibility. Go out there and make it, all of you. I want it epic, I want it tragic. I want it cheap.'

'Has he actually given it the go-ahead?' asked Henry anxiously, looking around for Cynthia Hyde-Lemon.

'I do believe he has, young man,' said Sir Luke Trimingham. 'You had better join us for dinner. Unless you have other arrangements. This is no evening for a ruined man to spend alone.'

'I don't think I do,' said Henry. 'A ruined man?'

'Of course,' said Sir Luke. 'You realise this moment marks the end of any career you might have hoped for as a serious writer? You understand the despite in which you will now be universally held? Let us go and get very, very drunk, young man. I have taken the wise precaution, as I do, of filling my pockets with wine.'

And Henry went. And, in the lounge of the best hotel in town, they did.

11

The following morning, with yet more to come on over the rest of the weekend, the couple of hundred brilliant people who were off to create *Serious Damage* set off in the arranged transportation, waving the cut-price airline tickets bought at cut-throat prices by Roger Trothammer's able and efficient organisational production team, for Heathrow airport, Switzerland, and Day One of the shooting schedule, starting at eight on the Monday morning.

They packed the airport and they packed the Swiss flights, chattering and teasing and laughing and screaming, for they were unusual travellers. They bottlenecked at immigration, and caused even more immense problems at security as they unloaded from their hand-luggage cameras and viewfinders, film-stock and fire-arms, and explosive fuses for blowing up houses in the more dramatic scenes. They went into the duty-free shops with their various cut-rate offers, and practically stripped them bare. They smoked in the non-smoking areas of the departure lounges, and when airport hostesses came and asked them to stop they tried to seduce them. They rocked the bus that drove them out to the plane. They occupied nearly all the seats on nearly all the Zürich flights, leading actors, directors, the camera-men and Lord Mellow up in first class, production and design in club, and make-up, costumes and speaking extras in economy; just as in life itself. They all ate three in-flight lunches apiece and then got up and danced in the aisles of the plane. They drank all the champagne on the drinks-trolleys, then begged the chief steward, who wore an unfortunate lapel badge saying *Die Airline*, to go outside and get some more.

At Zürich, they stumbled off the plane coughing as they stepped into the fresh Swiss air, stood in crowds in the Swiss customs loudly mocking Swiss customs, then poured through the well-conducted and polite airport buying kirsch, trying out cuckoo clocks, and swinging newly purchased cowbells. They made a terrible fuss as they tried to change not just pounds but krugerrands, Hungarian forints, and even articles of female under-clothing for the stable Swiss franc at the sober Swiss exchange desk, where money is taken extremely seriously. Big signs in the lobby said *Serious Damage: This Way* and, hooting and honking, they followed the directions to the concourse outside, where more transportation waited. There were big limousines with signs saying *S.D.* on them for Lord Mellow, the leading actors, the cameramen and the director, and big buses for the rest. Then the flotilla set off, led by a man on a motor-bicycle, through the green valleys, up into the wooded foothills, into the grey mountains and up past the snowline to Gstumbli, the high and exclusive Alpine resort where they would be working for the first few weeks of the shoot.

The cars and buses unloaded them into their accommodation. Leading actors, Lord Mellow, the director, the senior executives and the cameramen stayed at the world-famous, seven-star, incredibly exclusive Hotel Paradisohof, where even the swimming pool was a three-mile-long lake. Production and design, and people with small but speaking parts, stayed at the more modest

Hotel Ratskeller, where there was a smell of dumpling and a noisy bar. Make-up, costumes and non-speaking extras stayed at the ethnic and primitive Gasthof Bumli, which was a considerable vertical climb up the mountainside and entirely enveloped in cloud. The flotilla of Eldorado vans, containing all the carefully planned resources for the production, the props and the costumes and the generators and the portable toilets, which had set off from Britain some days before, had already arrived, except for one which had gone nose-down into a ravine. Happily it was laden only with contemporary costumes, which could easily be replaced at the very highest prices at the many designer boutiques in this chic resort location.

Once settled in, the *Serious Damage* team set out to make themselves comfortable. They booked tables for every night for the next month at all the local restaurants. They hired skis in case the weather changed from its present mild drizzling rain to crisp white snow. They set up telecommunications with Britain, the United States, Australia, Japan and Taiwan, they rented a bear and three handlers for the second week of the shoot, booked a mountainside, paid off the local police to let them park anywhere and do anything, made golfing arrangements some fifty miles away for Lord Mellow and Sir Luke Trimingham, and generally got down to making a major television series.

Henry did not in fact accompany them. It did occur to him to suggest that he could have been helpful from time to time, rewriting lines and explaining to people what the scripts actually meant when they said things; but Mark Hasper said that he did not allow writers on the set when he was working, and Roger Trothammer enthusiastically agreed. Henry had done his work, and now it was time for him to cut and run, go back to the village and the garden shed to find it in whatever state of neglect. He stayed in the great sad city over the weekend, to sleep off the farewell party and pack up his things. On Monday morning he went across to the Eldorado glass tower, to gather up what belongings he had there and depart. There was silence in the long corridor which had seen so much activity; the sign on the door saying *Serious Damage* had gone. The great office within was entirely empty, except for one person sitting at a desk in a far corner talking on the telephone, the big girl in knee-warmers, whose job nobody seemed to know or understand.

Henry went to his desk and began throwing piles of discarded script into the wastepaper basket, and putting a few treasures like his Remington Portable into boxes. The girl in the kneewarmers put down the telephone and then it rang again.

'Yes, Lord Mellow,' she said. 'He's here.' She waved at Henry. 'It's Lord Mellow on the line from Gstumbli. He wants to talk to you. I don't think his temper is very good.'

'Hello,' said Henry into the phone.

'I want you,' said Lord Mellow. 'I want you here in this hotel right away. I want you on the plane in an hour. I want you up this fucking mountain by teatime.'

'I've already ...' said Henry.

'I don't care if you've an audience with the Queen, I want you here,' said Lord Mellow. 'I want you on the first shuttle out of town, and I want you on the first flight to Zürich out of Heathrow. I'd send my helicopter for you but it's in for service. Now put that stupid girl in the office back on the phone and I'll tell her how to fix it. She comes with you, is that clear?'

'Is there some problem?' asked Henry.

'I'll say there's a problem,' said Lord Mellow. 'There's one great atomic bomb of a problem. Now you get moving right away and I'll have a car at the airport with its engine running for you when you arrive. Just look for a sign saying *Serious Damage*. Now, give me the girl.'

'There's a problem,' explained Henry to the girl in kneewarmers. 'We have to get out to Switzerland right away.'

'Do you have your passport?' asked the girl, taking the telephone from him. 'Yes, Lord Mellow ...'

After that a great many things happened, all in a confusing and cut-up sort of way. For instance:

1/1. INT. PHOTO-BOOTH. DAY.

B., A MAN SMALL RATHER THAN TALL, SOMEWHERE BETWEEN THIRTY AND SIXTY, SITS IN THE BOOTH LOOKING AT THE PASSPORT PHOTO CAMERA. HE IS CLEARLY WORRIED ABOUT THE FUTURE. HE HAS A TRAVEL BAG OVER HIS SHOULDER. THE SOUND OF TROLLEYS AND AN ANNOUNCEMENT FOR A SPECIAL OFFER ON ANDREX INDICATES THAT THIS IS A CUT-PRICE SUPERMARKET.

A FEMALE VOICE CALLS ANGRILY FROM OUTSIDE THE BOOTH.

THE MAN TURNS. THE CAMERA FLASHES.

CUT TO:

1/2. EXT. TARMAC, LONDON AIRPORT. DAY.

A PLANE, ITS DOORS CLOSED, ABOUT TO TAKE OFF.
A SMALL VAN HURRIES ACROSS THE TARMAC.
THE VAN STOPS.
THE MAN, B., GETS OUT, FOLLOWED BY A WOMAN, X.
THE PLANE'S PASSENGER DOOR IS PUSHED OPEN
FROM WITHIN AND STEPS ARE LOWERED. B. AND X.
HURRY UP THE STEPS.
CUT TO:

1/3. INT. PLANE IN FLIGHT. DAY.

THE MAN, B., SITS IN A SEAT IN A CROWDED PLANE.
THE WOMAN, X., SITS NEXT TO HIM, POURS WHISKY
IN A PLASTIC GLASS, HANDS IT TO HIM.
B. FROM X.'S POV. HE IS FRANTIC.
X. FROM B.'S POV. SHE IS FAT BUT ATTRACTIVE.
CUT TO:

1/4. INT. ZURICH AIRPORT. DAY.

THE ARRIVALS LOBBY WITH PASSENGERS COMING
THROUGH. A LOUDSPEAKER VOICE OVER ANNOUN-
CES THE ARRIVAL OF THE BA FLIGHT FROM LONDON.
AN ATMOSPHERE OF INDESCRIBABLE BUSTLE.
A MAN, S., HOLDS UP A SIGN AND WATCHES THE
PASSENGERS. THE SIGN SAYS *SERIOUS DAMAGE.*
THE MAN, B., COMES OUT OF ARRIVALS, FOLLOWED
BY THE WOMAN, X.
THEY SEE THE SIGN AND GO OVER TO THE MAN S.
THE MAN S. GOES TOWARD THE EXIT.
B. FOLLOWS S.
X. FOLLOWS S. AND B.
AN ATMOSPHERE OF TOTAL CONFUSION.

CUT TO:

'Jesus, what kept you, Harold, I wanted you here by teatime,' said Lord Mellow in his totally palatial suite with lakeside view at the Hotel Paradisohof. 'Now we're on to champagne. What the hell do you think you're doing, keeping us standing around like this all day?'

In fact Lord Mellow was not standing at all, but lying face down on a massage table having his buttocks kneaded by a pretty masseuse. But Joss and Rog, Cyn and Mark were all standing around in the large sitting room, holding champagne glasses and wearing expressions of extreme gloom.

'It wasn't easy,' said Henry, putting down his travel bag. 'I had to get a temporary passport.'

'We don't work in television because it's easy,' said Lord Mellow. 'Do we, Cynthia? We work in television because it's one endless, unremitting, hopeless cock-up. God, man, you mean to tell me that you're a world-famous writer and you don't carry your passport with you at all times?'

'I came as soon as I could,' said Henry. 'On the next flight after the next flight.'

'I'd fire you, Harold, if I didn't need you,' said Lord Mellow. 'That's two whole hours of shooting lost. I ought to bill you for it, but I don't suppose you could pay. A hardened professional writer like you ought to know you can't keep a ten-million-pound production hanging around while you fart about looking for your passport.'

'Lord Mellow is upset,' said Cynthia Hyde-Lemon.

'I bear the world on my shoulders and the world lets me down,' said Lord Mellow. 'Harold, just get us out of this mess.'

'What mess?' said Henry.

'Mark, tell him about the mess,' said Lord Mellow.

'Don't make me do everything.'

'We started with some location shooting at eight this morning,' said Mark Hasper.

'He knows that,' said Lord Mellow. 'He's read the schedule.'

'It's the scene outside the psychiatric clinic in episode eleven,' said Mark.

'He remembers the scene,' said Lord Mellow. 'He wrote it.'

'We found the ideal location, there's a very famous clinic right down the street,' said Roger Trothammer.

'Jonquil Pouvoir is waiting for her father to come out,' said Mark Hasper.

'She walks up and down outside,' said Cynthia.

'She stops,' said Joss Pride.

'She looks round,' said Mark Hasper.

'She makes a decision,' said Cynthia Hyde-Lemon.

'She goes in,' said Mark Hasper.

'Yes?' said Henry.

'She went in,' said Mark Hasper, 'and they took one look and wouldn't let her out again.'

'It turns out she's three times round the twist,' said Lord Mellow. 'Whoever cast the nutcase in that part should take a dive off that mountain out there. And right away.'

'They kept her in?' said Henry.

'They locked her up and put the key away in an unnumbered safe-deposit,' said Lord Mellow. 'I want that character written out of the script immediately.'

'But she's the major character,' said Henry. 'That's the main part. She's one of the muscles of the story.'

'Exactly, Harold,' said Lord Mellow. 'That's why we need you.'

111

'Why not get another actress?' asked Henry.

'Do you know a world-famous actress who could step into a major role like that?' asked Mark Hasper. 'We tried, but there's nobody could take it on in less than a month.'

'Look, Harold, do you realise what it means when a star poops out on a major production?' said Lord Mellow. 'My Swiss backers are very cautious people. That's how they succeed where we fail. They want me to cut the whole thing. Chop it, cancel the project completely. I've said, just give us one chance, fellows. We've got a world-famous writer on this, and he'll fix it.'

'I see,' said Henry. 'We couldn't just delay the shooting for a while?'

'That girl – oh God, some girl, she's pushing sixty – is going to have electricity running through her head for the next two years,' said Lord Mellow. 'They'll have renewed the franchises by then. Harold, I want that lady out, right out. Cut. Eliminated. Shredded. Pulped. I want that story completely restructured so that no one could ever know she was even in it.'

'We'll lose all the female interest,' said Cynthia Hyde-Lemon.

'Okay, write in a seductive female who fits into the scenes we shoot after week four,' said Lord Mellow. 'But get this part right out of the script.'

'The problem is,' said Henry, 'the story entirely depends on what she finds out.'

'Don't come to me with problems, Harold,' said Lord Mellow. 'I have enough of my own. There are plenty of people in the story who can do the finding out. There's a cast of eighty out there. Let one of them do it. The Swiss mountain guide. The banker cousin from Geneva.'

'It wouldn't work,' said Henry.

'I don't care what you do,' said Lord Mellow. 'Let Sir Luke Trimingham die for longer. But get to those rewrites, Harold, they're written into your contract. I have it in my pocket. And my goddam passport. Okay, there's a typewriter set up in my bedroom. I want it epic, I want it dramatic, I want it functional, and I want it in the morning.'

'What scene do we shoot in the morning?' said Cynthia Hyde-Lemon.

'Lord Bourdalou's deathbed,' said Mark Hasper.

'Okay, don't make any changes to that, it's sacred,' said Lord Mellow. 'The rest you can fool with. Brad will help you. Mark will help you. Joss will help you. Cyn will help you. We'll all help you. Get in there and we'll have room service send you up a sandwich. It's time we all went down to dinner.'

There was dancing on the terrace that night at the Hotel Paradisohof. Beautiful people in Gucci and Pierre Cardin evening-wear laughed and flirted. In the restaurant everyone was eating Beluga caviar. The small and exclusive Palm Court orchestra was conducted by Solti. Waiters in gold coats poured ten-star brandy over steaks beside the damask-covered tables and set it on fire. Sir Luke Trimingham saw Joan Collins at another table and was persuaded by her to rise and recite Hamlet's soliloquy to the diners. At the next table a Greek entrepreneur bought an airline over a cheese fondue. Beautiful Russian spies flirted with German diplomats and acquired major state secrets in exchange for the promise of exotic favours. Princes from oil-rich Arab states met and later that night went to bed with famous stars from the Hollywood brat pack. Nigel Dempster sat in a corner taking notes. Mark Thatcher came in but did not stay long. Caspar Weinberger sat with Edvard Shevardnadze at a table in the Regine's nightclub downstairs practising the Gorbachev-style orange-juice diplomacy, and by midnight they had worked out a new deep cut in nuclear weaponry.

But Henry saw none of this. He had some deep cuts to make himself. In Lord Mellow's vast suite, which had an original Rembrandt on the wall, he worked, with scissors and paste and sellotape and tippex. He worked and worked, worked as he had never worked before. The elimination of Jonquil Pouvoir meant that in nearly all the major scenes the characters talked to someone who wasn't there about things that had not now happened, and the script was now two episodes too short.

The others did not greatly help, though they looked in after dinner from time to time. Cynthia Hyde-Lemon seemed to have lost all interest in his muscles, and left for bed very early, jangling her room-key in the direction of Joss Pride, who left himself shortly after. Mark Hasper apologised and said he had to make some important telephone calls to Hollywood about a Robert Redford project he just wanted to check on. Lord Mellow disappeared with the masseuse and did not return at all throughout the night. Brad said he was coming down with writer's cramp, and went off to bed. Only the big girl with the kneewarmers stayed and was any use at all, running downstairs for canapés and tippex and making some quite useful suggestions.

A great white moon came up over the Alps. Snow, great glaciers and the deep lake under the windows shone in its light. A fine high peak reached up into magenta clouds. There seemed to be wolves howling up

114

by the snowline. As Henry worked and worked, he began to notice something. It was as if a strange, obscure, silent flavour had entered the script now that Jonquil Pouvoir had exited from it. Once she had gone, there was no longer any need for anyone to explain anything to anyone. For a love-story there was now a notable shortage of people for people to fall in love with, so that it all had to be about something quite different. Perhaps it didn't really need to be about anything at all, or not in the sense of about that is usually about. Lots of events happened, but they happened disconnectedly, obscurely, just as in his novels. Indeed everything now had a decidedly Beckettian quality. Henry stopped his pasting and cutting. The girl in the kneewarmers, ever more helpful, whose job in life nobody knew up to now, turned out to be a trained speed typist, and was able to type up everything he said from his dictation. Together they went through the huge script, exploring its vacancies and spaces, writing in its margins. When his characters needed to talk, Henry let them talk to almost anything: to trees, animals, furniture, flowers, and mirrors: especially mirrors. But much of the time he allowed them silence. They sat in large hotel bedrooms writing silently while great parties and feasts went on within earshot below. They went out silently to look at great glaciers in the moonlight, or to row at night in a boat on the lake under the silent stars. They climbed pencil-slim mountain peaks while in the tundra wolves howled.

The sun came up over the tops of the mountains, staining the snow on the peaks above them red. Henry wrote that in too, making it the last shot. Then, silently, from his POV, he looked at X., over the typewriter. From her POV she turned, silently, and looked at B. There was no doubt about it; there was definitely an atmosphere of erotic anticipation. B. went out into the corridor and put out the sign that said *Do Not Disturb* on the door. It was Lord Mellow's suite; but he had, after all, always respected the writer.

12

In a delightful old wooden sanatorium in the chalet style, on the very top of a Swiss mountain, splendidly cut off by forest, fog and an ancient rack-railway from the commonplace world below, dear old Lord Bourdalou was about to breathe his last.

In the chair beside his vast bed sat a nice old nurse, reading *Cosmopolitan* and whistling Pink Floyd songs. Outside beside the antlered door stood Wolf, the loyal old Swiss mountain guide who had once saved Lord Bourdalou's life on the Eiger, forty years before, by cutting a rope at a particularly crucial moment. These two men had together shared Felicity, in her feckless youth, but Felicity was in London at the moment and in a production at the National Theatre and so could not be on the mountain too. Wolf was an old man now, so two amusing girls were putting a wig on him that – as one of them said – made him look definitely past his peak. Nearby stood Fritz, Wolf's son, a successful Swiss financier whom he had not seen for at least twenty years. He wore a business suit and carried a Samsonite briefcase and was talking to a man in jogging clothes and a sweatband round his head who said he actually was a Swiss banker. Fritz kept looking round, perhaps for Hermione, the love of his life, Lord Bourdalou's daughter. But Hermione was not there today, mostly because she was safely locked up in a real Swiss sanatorium down in Gstumbli in the valley below.

Inside the room where Lord Bourdalou lay in his vast

white bed, various things were happening. Someone turned bright lights on him and someone else held a tape-measure to the end of his nose. A great number of photographers went round taking photographs of Lord Bourdalou in his nigh mortal state. On the opposite side of the bed from the nurse, a man rode up and down on a little trolley on rails and kept looking at the dying man through a lens. Two pretty girls approached the dying man. One started painting the ashen grey colour of death into his cheeks, and the other drew a gelatinous dribble of saliva down his chin.

'Oh, my dears,' said the dying Lord Bourdalou, 'I cannot tell you how much I've been looking forward to this scene. Olivier has had one, you know, and Gielgud can boast of several. They set a standard in rigor mortis that will be hard to beat. But I have always been known to rise to a challenge. Oh, I shall be stimulating. I shall be affecting. I shall tug at your heart strings.'

'Stop it, Sir Luke,' said one of the girls, as old Lord Bourdalou pulled at the strings that held the top of her dress together. 'You're spoiling your dribble.'

'Oh, Charles,' said the fading, failing Lord Bourdalou to the focus puller who was holding the tape at the end of his nose, 'let me tell you how I shall do it, dear boy. The secrets of the trade. I shall gasp at the end. I shall rise half-erect, if you will pardon the expression. Then I shall sink back, very very slowly. My mouth will fall wide. My eyes will glaze. There will be a last cry, 'Felicity!' My head will fall sideways. I take it you'll close-up then.'

'Count on us, squire,' said the focus puller.

'Oh, nurse, nurse,' said poor old Lord Bourdalou. 'When I gasp and you lean forward and say the line asking me what I need, don't put your head in front of mine. Remember I'm about to deliver a three-page dying speech, and I want my expression properly established.'

'You're a mean old bugger, Sir Luke,' said the nurse.

Henry stood on the edge of the set and watched all this, one of about fifty people who had come up the mountain this morning to see dear old Lord Bourdalou shuffle off his mortal coil. He was already finding that location shooting was very boring and consisted mostly of not shooting at all, and there was little for a world-famous writer to do. Moreover few people ever came to speak to him, having more interesting things to do with their lives, like holding up tape measures and reading *Cosmopolitan*.

'Sir Luke seems to be enjoying himself greatly,' said Joss Pride, coming over. 'Well, Henry, this is your big final scene.'

'Why are we shooting it first?' asked Henry.

'Because it fits in with the Swiss schedule,' said Joss Pride.

'I wrote it for an English country house,' said Henry.

'I remember,' said Joss. 'Somewhere like Castle Howard but bigger, I think you said. But if we shoot the whole thing with Swiss backers on a continental location we don't have to pay British tax.'

'He's supposed to be a faithful ghillie, not a Swiss mountain guide,' said Henry.

'The Swiss backers demanded some Swiss actors,' said Joss Pride.

'It's supposed to happen in the worst blizzard of the century,' said Henry.

'Don't worry, Henry,' said Joss Pride, 'it will.'

'Henry, get out of the way, you're in shot,' said Mark Hasper. 'Quiet please. Going for a take.'

Philip, the first assistant director, began talking over

his two-way radio to various invisible people who were evidently stationed outside.

'Give me the blizzard,' he said.

There was a tumult beyond the windows as some marvellous piece of production technology started up and the bright sunny day turned into a whirligig of snowflakes.

'Snow throwers, start throwing the snow,' said Philip.

Some men who must have been lying under the windows began throwing artificial snow into the air.

'Give me wind,' said Philip.

Another machine stationed just outside the sanatorium began making windy noises.

'Okay, now, good luck. Let's mark it,' said Mark Hasper.

A girl with a clapperboard ran forward, clapped it, and said, 'Scene four, take one.'

In the bed, Lord Bourdalou's mouth fell gapingly, convincingly open. He gasped. He groaned. He waved feebly toward the nurse, who sat in the chair by his bed.

'What is it, my lord?' asked the nurse.

'Bring me ...' stammered Lord Bourdalou, 'bring me ... Hermione.'

'She can't, can she? She's in the nuthouse,' shouted Mark Hasper. 'Cut cut cut.'

'That is the line,' said Sir Luke Trimingham. 'I always study my scripts very carefully, bathetic though they may be.'

'I know it's the line,' said Mark Hasper. 'Where's Henry, where's the writer? I thought that character had been cut.'

Henry came forward, pleased to have something to do.

'Lord Mellow said this scene was sacred,' he said. 'He

told me not to touch it.'

'Well, touch it now,' said Mark Hasper. 'The old bugger's dying and he needs someone to speak the three-page speech you wrote him to. He has to ask for someone who exists. Who does he ask for?'

Henry looked round and saw Wolf the old Swiss guide standing watching in a corner of the set.

'Wolf, the old Swiss mountain guide,' he said.

'Hans-Joachim, come over here,' said Mark Hasper. 'This is your big opportunity, Hansie, *ja?*'

'*Ja*,' said Wolf the old Swiss guide.

'You can have all Hermione's lines, she doesn't need them any more,' said Mark Hasper. 'Just check they all make sense. You understand me, Hansie?'

'Sure, fine, *ja ja*, is good, I take them,' said Wolf the old Swiss guide, leaning on his alpenstock.

'Okay,' said Mark Hasper.

'Blizzard, snow throwers, wind,' said Philip to his walkie-talkie.

'Mark it,' said Mark Hasper.

'Scene four, take two,' said the clapperboard girl.

'What is it?' said the nurse.

'Bring me ... bring me my old friend Wolf,' said Lord Bourdalou.

'Here I am, daddy,' said the old Swiss guide, coming into shot.

'Cut cut cut,' shouted Mark Hasper. 'He's not your daddy.'

'In the scriptus it tells daddy,' said the old Swiss guide.

'Okay, take a break. Henry, Henry, get over here,' shouted Mark Hasper.

'Yes?' said Henry.

'Henry, sit down with that stupid bugger and clean up

his lines,' said Mark Hasper. 'And see Sir Luke gets the rewrites as well.'

Henry sat down with the old Swiss guide and began to change his lines. Working on location was very boring, but perhaps the writer did have a few useful things to add now and then, apart from rewriting the entire script overnight. He looked up and saw that Lord Mellow had come in and was watching, along with the four Swiss bankers who accompanied him everywhere and were now looking at their Japanese watches and using pocket calculators.

'I see I shall be a long time a-dying,' said Sir Luke. 'Has anyone got today's *Times?*'

'Not up here,' said Mark Hasper. 'Hurry up, Henry. Right? Ready? Let's go.'

'Blizzard, snow-throwing, wind,' said Philip to the people outside.

'Mark it,' said Mark Hasper.

'Scene four, take three,' said the clapperboard girl.

'What is it?' said the nurse.

'Bring me ... bring me Wolf,' said Lord Bourdalou.

'Here I am, mein gut old freund,' said Wolf the old Swiss guide, coming into shot.

'Ah, Wolf, Wolf,' murmured Lord Bourdalou. 'Wolf who saved my life on the mountain. What is it like now, Wolf, out there on the mountain ...?'

Out there on the mountain there suddenly started an extremely unpleasant noise, of whirring and screeching, carving and scouring. It bounced off the peaks. It echoed through the valleys. It resounded through the set.

'Cut cut cut cut cut,' shouted Mark Hasper. 'What the hell is that? That's not one of our effects.'

'What the hell is that?' asked Philip on the walkie-talkie. 'I don't believe it. Mark, they've started cutting down the forest on the other side of the ravine.'

'They can't do that,' said Mark Hasper. 'Don't they know we're shooting a major television project?'

'Nobody thought it could happen,' said Philip, 'but apparently the forest is dying of acid rain. They'll be cutting it down for weeks.'

'Then send someone over there to tell them to stop,' shouted Mark Hasper. 'Pay them whatever it takes. Buy the forest if necessary. How long will we have to wait?'

'About an hour,' said Philip, after he had consulted his walkie-talkie. 'He's got to go right down the valley and up the other side.'

'Okay, everybody, take a nice long break,' said Mark Hasper. 'This is just our schedule going to pieces, after all. Have breakfast, take a walk, get some fresh air. We can close down here, put out the lights.'

'I see we are in for a very long day's shoot,' said Sir Luke. 'May I take off this depressing make-up?'

'Please do, Sir Luke,' said Cynthia Hyde-Lemon, coming over. 'I'm terribly sorry about these delays.'

'Don't concern yourself, my dear,' said Sir Luke, patting her hand. 'My contract gives me extraordinarily substantial sums if we go into overtime. Now tell me, young lady, how did I do?'

'Wonderfully, Sir Luke,' said Cynthia Hyde-Lemon.

'I thought so too,' said Sir Luke. 'Don't you think we have the prospect of a most gratifying climax?'

'A terrific climax,' said Cynthia Hyde-Lemon.

'Do you think so, my dear?' said Sir Luke thoughtfully. 'May I discuss some of my thoughts on the scene with you?'

'Of course, Sir Luke,' said Cynthia Hyde-Lemon, sitting

123

on the bed. 'You mean about muscles and things.'

'I do indeed,' said Sir Luke.

It was clear that nothing in the least interesting was going to happen for some long time, so Henry left the set and went out into the winey mountain air. Lord Mellow stood in a snowdrift with the Swiss bankers, who were talking to him energetically. Most of the cast and the crew were gathered by the refreshment truck, eating bacon and beans, which they seemed to do most of the time when they were not actually working. They appeared as oblivious of the natural wonders around them as they were of him. There was a little track across the ridge, for mountain walkers, and Henry took it. Fog and cloud lay in the great valley below, and from it emerged the hideous whirr of the great cutting machines that were tearing down the forest, and the lumbering crash of falling trees. But above were the high peaks of the Alps, pure and white, calm and indifferent, just like a world-famous writer. Henry climbed upward toward them, growing breathless in the rarified air. Then, suddenly, the noise from the valley below stopped. The Eldorado emissary had evidently done his work, and shooting would be starting again. Henry turned and began to hurry back toward the sanatorium, through the little graveyard at the back, and into the large wooden building, long closed until it had been reopened for the purposes of *Serious Damage*.

When he returned to the great deathbed room, the lights were on again, but somehow the set-up seemed mysteriously to have changed. Lord Bourdalou lay again on his deathbed. There was an ashen colour of death on his cheeks. A dribble of saliva ran down his chin. His mouth gaped hideously open. His eyes were glazed. But this time Cynthia Hyde-Lemon was also in the bed. She seemed to be naked, apart from a sheet pulled carelessly around her, and she was crying dreadfully. The photographers were taking a lot of photographs.

'I'm sorry,' she said, 'I just had no idea he was likely to over-exert himself. He seemed remarkably fit and vital for a man of his age when we started.'

'Maybe he had a problem with the atmosphere,' said Philip, the first assistant director, consolingly. 'We're over a mile high up here. Never mind, Cyn. He couldn't have wished for a better exit.'

'He did say he wanted the series to go out with a bang,' said Michael, the second assistant director.

'He always wanted to do the best of the great deathbed scenes,' said Dick, the third assistant director.

'Jesus, what's happened here?' asked Lord Mellow, coming in.

'It's Sir Luke,' said Mark Hasper. 'He died in the act.'

'Did we shoot it?' asked Lord Mellow.

'It wouldn't have been suitable,' said Mark Hasper.

'Jesus, I don't believe it,' said Lord Mellow, turning to the Swiss bankers. 'I want whoever's responsible dunked in a bath of acid.'

Cynthia Hyde-Lemon started to cry very loudly.

'I want the corpse off the set and I want it buried quietly and as quickly as possible,' said Lord Mellow. 'If with dignity. I want a doctor to certify he died of over-exerting himself at the lavatory. I want no word of this in the press and I want everyone here sworn to total secrecy. I want this scene cleared and I want everybody in my suite tonight to see what we can salvage from this cursed production. And I want Harold.'

'Henry,' said Henry.

'Henry,' said Lord Mellow. 'My dear young man, can you ...?'

'I very much doubt it,' said Henry.

'Not if we gave you a double fee?' asked Lord Mellow. 'Not if we bought you a gold word-processor? Henry, there's a ten-million-pound investment at stake.'

'He was the other muscle,' said Henry.

Late that night, in his palatial suite at the Hotel Paradisohof, Lord Mellow sat in his bed in his pyjamas, wearing a black armband, and held his meeting. His four Swiss bankers – Franz Stubli of the Züger Brugerbank, Hans Frumli of the Züricher Volkscredit, Max Patli of the Bruger Zügerbank, and Jean-Luc Ruber of the Crédit Mauvais de Genève – were there by his side. So were Henry and Joss and Brad and Mark and Philip and Michael and Dick. Cyn was in her room sobbing. And nobody, for some time, had seen Roger Trothammer.

'What are we going to do?' asked Lord Mellow. 'Henry's been giving me negative signals. One of our major stars is in the nuthouse and the other is in the morgue. We've got nothing to shoot, nobody to shoot with, and we're half way through the budget already. And I can't find Roger Trothammer.'

'There's an unfortunate rumour about him we've not been able to confirm,' said Joss Pride. 'One of the drivers took him into Zurich yesterday. He asked to be driven to one of the Swiss banks that specialise in unnumbered accounts. Then he wanted to go to the airport. He never returned to the car, so the driver went and looked around. He thought he saw him embarking in rather good humour on the night flight to Ecuador.'

'Has anyone checked the production account in the hotel safe?' asked Lord Mellow.

'It's gone,' said Joss Pride apologetically.

'Jump off the balcony, Joss,' said Lord Mellow, and he turned to the bankers. 'Well, there you have it, gentlemen. As shrewd financiers, economic wizards, I'd welcome your expert advice. In the circumstances, do we go ahead or do we not?'

The bankers turned to look at each other, opened their code-locked briefcases, and said nothing for some time.

'Perhaps in the macro-economical climate there are more advantageous investings than a major televisional sequence,' said Franz Stubli at last, rather slowly.

'Investment prospects are changing most vastly now in London you like to be having your very big bang,' said Max Patli.

'Aussi il-y-a une chose nouvelle de conséquence, le projet TSB,'' said Jean-Luc Ruber.

'So in words other we like to advise perhaps you cut your losses,' said Hans Frumli.

So Lord Mellow, in bed in his black armband, made his decision; and the television series that would, if it had been made, probably have been called *Serious Damage* was – well, not to put too fine a point on it, cut.